MW01422377

THE WOLF OF CLASS 1D

By M.D. Tolman

*The Wolf of Class 1D Copyright © 2018 by M.D. Tolman.
All rights reserved. Printed in the United States of America. No part of this book may be used or reproduced in any manner whatsoever without written permission except in the case of brief quotations embodied in critical articles or reviews.*

This book is a work of fiction. Names, characters, businesses, organizations, places, events and incidents either are the product of the author's imagination or are used fictitiously. Any resemblance to actual persons, living or dead, events, or locales is entirely coincidental.

For information contact; www.malcolmtolman.com

*Book and Cover design by Melissa Tolman
Images Used Under License From cynoclub/shutterstock.com
Cover Brushes From Brusheezy.com*

*© 2018 Lulu Author. All rights reserved.
ISBN: 978-1-387-50124-3*

*First Edition: January 2018
10 9 8 7 6 5 4 3 2 1*

*This book is dedicated to all who feel things deeply.
May the world never call your sensitivity weakness.*

CHAPTER ONE
Welcome the Wolf _____ 8

CHAPTER TWO
A New Perspective _____ 20

CHAPTER THREE
Swords and Armor _____ 38

CHAPTER FOUR
Tangled Vines _____ 48

CHAPTER FIVE
Allies and Burdens _____ 60

CHAPTER SIX
The First Job _____ 68

CHAPTER SEVEN
The Pervert _____ 82

CHAPTER EIGHT
The Collar Breaks _____ 94

CHAPTER NINE
Times Change _____ 108

CHAPTER TEN
The Dragon and the Phoenix _____ 116

CHAPTER ELEVEN
Reconciliation _____ 126

CHAPTER TWELVE
The Death of a Rabbit _____ 138

CHAPTER THIRTEEN
All Together _____ 148

> # CHAPTER ONE
Welcome the Wolf

My name is Miyaki Mei, a student born and raised in a small town off the coast of Japan.

For the last fifteen years my life had been boring, empty, average, but that was all about to change. Because now, I was finally in high school!

High School! The time of new friendships! Exciting adventures! Club activities! Thrilling romances! And much, much more!

The days of mediocrity were finally behind me, and a new life of passion awaited. There was just one little problem...

"My life is so boring!" I groaned as I let my head fall defeated on my desk.

For more than two months now my life had repeated the same monotonous cycle.

I would wake up early, get ready, eat a simple breakfast, sit through classes, eat lunch with my friends, sit through more classes, go home alone, do my homework... occasionally, go to bed, and then the whole cycle would repeat.

I never joined a club, never volunteered as class rep, never received a love confession in my shoe locker.

The seat in the back of class next to the window where most *manga* protagonists would sit remained empty, while I found myself seated in the center of class like any old background character.

My high school days were quickly disappearing, and here I was with nothing to show for it!

"What's wrong, Mei?" I heard a peppy but worried voice call out. "Why the long face?"

Looking up, I was met by a face with a large pair of brown eyes, cute nose, and concerned frown invading my personal bubble.

It was my best friend Aki. She was a short ball of energy with a ponytail, who was almost always smiling. From track team to the classroom, she was considered a ray of sunshine wherever she went.

Behind her stood another friend. A taller, tan girl with short brown hair named Miyori.

While Aki was cute and energetic, Miyori was mature and level-headed. To some, she was mistaken for being strict or cold, but she had a gentle, nurturing nature to her which always seemed to draw people back.

"I dunno." I sighed as I stretched. "Don't you find our high school lives are turning out to be a bit of a letdown?"

The two shared a confused glance between each other before they gave their reply.

"No," Miyori stated.

"Not really…" Aki agreed.

"You guys!" I groaned lowering my head to my desk once again.

"Ah sorry Mei!" Aki consoled awkwardly. "It's just I've been so busy with clubs and helping teachers that I really haven't had the time to feel bored yet!"

Miyori placed a firm hand on my shoulder as she looked at me with a sage expression.

"Fate favors the industrious. If you want the exciting high school life you've always read about, you need to chase after it yourself!"

My blank, unimpressed stare was apparently not enough to discourage her as she continued, "Join a club! Try some sports! Or take the time to actually study for a change!"

I buried my head deeper into my arms as she brought up my studies. I had never been the best student, nor the most athletic. And did I really want to become 'The girl that did nothing but study all day?' ...No, I really did not.

Miyori patted my head in consolation.

"Life won't just throw adventure at you, you know," she pointed out in a gentle tone.

Deep down, I knew there was wisdom in her words, but at the same time, I wasn't about to accept that. Before my groan of disappointment could escape my lips however, our energetic teacher, Ms. Koba walked into class.

"All right, ya hooligans! Everyone sit down!" she called out in her usual rough manner. It had taken a while for our class to adapt to her laid-back tone and aggressive demeanor, but now her colloquialisms were considered a natural part of our school routine.

"Soo uhh... I know this is sort of short notice," she explained while scratching her head, "but we have a transfer student comin' today. He ain't from around here, so be kind to him, show him around, don't make fun of how his Japanese ain't like yours. All that sort of stuff."

The class began to murmur as the teacher turned towards the door.

An exchange student! And a *gaijin* as well! The thought of taking classes with a foreigner was nerve wracking, but also exciting. Could this be the start to the adventure I had been waiting for?

I could see it all coming together in my mind.

He would come into my life, a tall, dark, handsome man. He would have chiseled features, thick blond hair, blue eyes, and have a deep and charming voice.

First, he would ask me to show him around the school, during which our relationship would start to blossom. From there, he would ask if I could direct him around town. Explain our customs. We might even get caught in the rain and... have to share an umbrella together! I blushed at the thought.

We would be awkward, but respectful of each other. He would find everything I talk about rich and fascinating, and I would find everything he talked about new and exciting.

Over time, in order to communicate better, we would help each other with our language studies. He would be adorable yet studious as he stumbled through his Japanese, and then he would be patient and intimate as he taught me English.

Slowly but surely as we shared more experiences and gained more memories together, there would come the day when he, blushing, would ask me how to say 'I love you' in Japanese. And that would be the start of our beautiful relationship. Traveling all around the world, having new adventures every day, and—

I looked up to see the teacher standing next to a short, scrawny boy with unkempt shaggy hair. His pants were already torn and he was wearing a wrinkled, untucked shirt. His squinty eyes were almost brown with a slight hint of green in them, accented by the sickly dark circles underneath. His complexion was pale and unhealthy looking, and he looked like a middle schooler.

It seemed that hygiene products such as a brush were a foreign concept to him. Instead of a tie, he wore a black pendant around his neck similar to an army dog tag, that had 'Courage' poorly etched into it in Japanese.

"Well go on and introduce yourself." Ms. Koba exclaimed as she slapped him on the back, causing him to nearly fall over.

With a slight adjustment of his slouched posture, he mumbled.

"Yo! The name's Finn. Finn Coller. I'm from Canada. Nice to meetchya!"

You're kidding... I thought to myself as I analyzed this major letdown standing before me.

I had heard that *gaijin* were more casual than Japanese people, but this was ridiculous! And weren't they all supposed to be tall in other countries? This boy looked like he would barely reach my shoulder! He was possibly even shorter than Aki! And what was with that language? He sounded like he had come straight out of some *anime*! What kind of person would speak like that in real life?

The faces around the class mirrored various states of confusion and disappointment, as the teacher pointed to the empty desk near the window at the back.

As Finn turned towards his seat, a new voice broke out.

"Oye teach! Is this some kind of sick joke?!" the menacing voice called out from the back of the class. "What are we doing letting some big-headed *gaijin* come in here and act like he owns the place?"

No one needed to look. We all recognized the voice right away. It was Tanaka Shoma, the class' self-proclaimed 'delinquent'.

"I got told off just last week for not wearing my tie tight enough, and now this guy gets to come in here looking like he crawled out of a dumpster?" He continued his rant as he stood up at his desk. "And what's with that introduction huh? I bet you're looking down on us aren't ya *gaijin*! You think you're better than us, just because you come from some English-speaking country don't ya!"

People shifted uneasily in their chairs, not wanting to make eye contact lest they get pulled into the awkward situation.

As confidentially as I could, I let my gaze wander towards the new kid. He may not have been anyone I'd ever be caught dead hanging out with, but I still felt bad about him having to deal with Tanaka on his first day.

It must have been awkward for him. I would have expected him to feel attacked and persecuted. I would have expected him to be wishing he had never come to Japan in the first place. That is what I would have expected, and that is why his actual expression caught me so off guard.

Finn stood completely expressionless. His face showed no signs of pain, anger, or even fear. His eyes seemed to be locked with Tanaka, yet he appeared to be almost bored.

What's with this guy, anyways? I thought as turned my eyes back down towards my desk.

This reaction seemed to agitate Tanaka even more. His face was red as he slammed his hands down on his desk, causing the sound to reverberate throughout the classroom.

"People from the west are always looking down on everyone else!" he shouted. "Constantly treating us like animals at a zoo, or suffering victims they need to save. Thinking they can do whatever they want as long as they throw money at it. You think this class is a vacation don't you!? Everyone in this class is just an experience for you to tell your rich-boy friends about aren't we!?"

This was going far, even for Tanaka. A member of the class cleared his throat uncomfortably.

"Oy, Tanaka!" Ms. Koba warned. "Hold your tongue before I come back there and deal with it myself!"

Tanaka spat in Finn's direction as he kicked his desk aside. The class watched in silence as Tanaka stomped towards the door.

"Tanaka!" Ms. Koba called out, trying to intercept him on the way out but it was too late.

The door slammed shut as Tanaka left, and the tension in the classroom grew far worse.

As if things weren't already awkward enough... I thought to myself as I buried my face in my arms.

Students shot awkward glances to one another as the teacher went to the door. The boys seemed to be debating who should take responsibility for Tanaka's actions, while the girls just seemed to be embarrassed to be a part of this class.

The only one who seemed unaffected by Tanaka's outburst was the student it had been directed at. As soon as the door had slammed shut, Finn made his way to his seat and pulled out his books for class, his bored expression barely changing.

"What is he? A statue?" one of the girls whispered.

"Dummy," another guy returned. "You heard his Japanese earlier didn't you? He probably didn't understand anything Tanaka said!"

"I guess Tanaka's accent would be difficult for a *gaijin*..." another student agreed.

For the first time since we had been introduced to her, Ms. Koba stood speechless.

"So, umm, yeah!" she cleared her throat at last, attempting to regain her composure. "Welcome to the class, Mr. Canada! Be sure ya ask your fellow students if ya need anything. I think it's about time we were starting on today's lessons."

With Ms. Koba's awkward transition, the class took out their textbooks and class resumed.

Students shifted uneasily in their seats and continued to exchange glances with each other.

Finn seemed oblivious to it all as he sat in his seat, gazing out the window beside him.

Do things like this happen often overseas? I wondered as my mind drifted away from the lecture. So much for my romantic adventure. This was turning out to be more of a disaster.

The Wolf of Class 1D

Class was boring and awkward. About halfway through I found my eyes wandering absently back towards my much-coveted back window seat. My gaze didn't last long however as I realized Finn, the seat's new occupant was staring straight towards me.

My eyes shot back to the front of the classroom as I attempted to hide my blushing face.

What was that?! I screamed internally as I held my hands against my burning cheeks. *He couldn't have been. I must have miss-seen it. Yes! That's right! I'm overreacting for nothing!*

Subtly, I let my eyes wander back to Finn's seat. They shot back to the front quickly however, as my horrors were confirmed.

What is with him!? I continued to panic as I began nervously running my fingers through my hair. *Why is he looking this way?!*

Does he have a thing for Japanese girls? Is he a stalker? I know they say they're more forward about love overseas but this is crazy! And why me? What did I do to stand out! Do I have something on my face? Did I look at him oddly? Did I do something insulting? What did I do to deserve this!?

Hiding my face behind my textbook I tried to ignore his gaze as I unsuccessfully attempted to focus on whatever the teacher was saying.

The rest of the day was a nightmare.

Tanaka never did return to class, not that anyone had expected him to. In spite of his absence, the tension he had left behind never seemed to dissipate. Only Finn seemed to be unaffected by it.

Even though Finn eventually stopped looking at me, I still wasn't certain how I felt about him. Everything about him seemed to push your attention away from him, even in an all-Japanese classroom where he should have stood out.

Others seemed to notice this as well, as any attempts to make conversation with him died out after two or three sentences. Eventually people got bored of trying and went back to their usual friends.

By the time the school day was over, I was completely exhausted. Like most days, Aki left early to go to track meet, and Miyori soon followed as she left for student council. With no club, I had no reason to stay after school, so I decided to head home early for the day.

"Man, what a day!" I sighed as I walked down the empty streets. "Lectures were boring, I did horrible on that test, and then THAT guy!"

I clenched my fist.

"What was with him?!" I cried out, kicking a rock down the road. "Stupid *gaijin*! Doesn't he know how to treat a lady? I don't know what they teach in Canada but manners are clearly no—"

A loud crash from the nearby alleyway stopped my solo tirade.

Oh shoot! I thought to myself covering my mouth. *Was there someone nearby? Did they hear me shouting?* I paused for a moment, but nothing happened.

Gathering my courage with a deep breath, I cautiously peered down into the dark alley.

"Hello?" I whispered. Still, there was no reaction.

It must have been a cat. I thought, as I turned my back to the alleyway.

As I began to walk away, a louder crash came from behind me, this time closer than before, sending a chill down my spine.

Turning around as fast as I could, I saw a figure hunched over some toppled garbage cans.

"Ta-Tanaka?!" I gasped as I recognized his face.

The lip piercing, the dyed blond hair, the various chains and studded bracelets. There was no doubting that it was Tanaka, but who had done this to him?

His face was filthy, his clothes were torn, and his arms had blood dripping down them.

"Tanaka! Are you all right!?" I cried out as I ran to his side. He may have been loud and violent, but he was still my classmate. The thought that someone might have attacked him was terrifying!

"Tanaka! What happened to you?" I asked as I helped him back up to his feet. "Who did this? Can you hear me?"

"Idiots…" Tanaka growled, almost too quietly for me to hear.

Before I could ask what he meant, I felt a sharp pain in my gut as the world around me began to turn. I felt as if I was flying. The next thing I knew I was lying on my back, a dull pain burning in my stomach. I wanted to cry out, but all the air had been forced out of my lungs.

"Ta-na-ka…" I struggled in a hoarse voice.

Something was wrong. I had to stop him! This wasn't the Tanaka I had seen in class! The Tanaka I knew was obnoxious, but was all bark and no bite. He quickly retreated when he realized he went too far and never really wanted to hurt anyone. The way he was acting now was more like a beast than a person.

I tried to focus on his hunched form, but my vision was blurring.

Not now, eyes! I thought to myself as I tried to force my vision to stay in focus. I felt like there was something important I was missing. I wanted to see it. I had to see it!

"Idiots! *Gaijin*! *Gaijin* lovers! Naive!" Tanaka continued, spitting out random words as if he was vomiting them out. As he continued, the air around him seemed to warp like steam above a road on a hot day.

"What… What's happening?" I coughed. The haze began growing thicker and larger around him.

The haze was morphing Tanaka's body. No; it was more as if a fog was lifting, revealing his true form which had been hidden.

The chains he wore grew in size, digging into his body. His arms grew longer and larger with massive blocky fists at the ends.

His eyes and nose were missing. In fact, most of his face was taken up by his large, monstrous mouth, filled with jagged fangs. Slobber dripped down his chin as thick as slime.

But the most noticeable change was his size. He was massive! He filled almost the entirety of the alleyway. It was as if his body had grown to match the size of his ego!

"Tanaka!" I sputtered, tears welling up in my eyes. "Stop it! Please! What's happening? This isn't you! Come back to us!"

I cried out as loud as I could. I called out about class memories, compliments, threats. I cried out with every response I could think of, but the massive creature before me no longer had any ears to hear with.

"IDIOTS!" the oversized mouth continued to scream as it pounded the walls with bleeding fists in a blind rage. The voice was so loud and thundering that I covered my ears in pain.

"Kill them! Kill them all! They don't deserve to live! They deserve to suffer! Suffer like we suffered! Let them suffer!

KILL THEM! KILL THEM! KILL THEM!!"

I tried to scream as a bloody fist the size of my body came flying towards me, but my diaphragm had still not recovered from the earlier blow.

Crying, I covered my eyes with my arm and braced myself for the incoming blow. But for some reason, the pain never came.

I reluctantly looked up as I felt something soft brush against my arm.

Something large and bushy was dangling in front of me, flipping left and right.

"A t-tail?" I managed to say as I lacked the strength to pick myself up off the ground.

Straining my eyes to look up one last time, I recognized the disheveled uniform of the student standing before me. He was from our school, but he was like no one I had ever seen before.

He had a long, bushy wolf-like tail, wore a thick, studded dog collar tightly around his neck, and to top it all off, he had two furry wolf ears on top of his head.

He held his arm raised above his head, clutching Tanaka's fist in a red, clawed hand.

"A…Wolf?" I asked, before my consciousness left me completely.

CHAPTER TWO

A New Perspective

A gentle breeze blew across my face, waking me from my slumber. My body was sore and stiff, and my head felt like it was ready to split in two.

"What... happened?" I groaned, rubbing my blurry eyes. I tried to get a sense of where I was, but my eyes were having trouble focusing.

Letting my hand fall to the ground, I realized I was lying on a grassy field. I could hear the sound of the ocean lapping against the coast a little ahead of me and the sky seemed to be red.

As my eyes finally began to clear, I realized I was lying on a hill overlooking the ocean. the sun was setting and most people had already gone home for the day. But what was I doing here and how did I get here?

Memories of the alleyway came flooding back into my head all at once, as I leapt to my feet.

"Tanaka!" I gasped shooting up straight. I began scanning the area, but he was nowhere to be seen. The garbage cans, the alleyway, that wolf-boy... I couldn't see any of that now.

What I did see however, was a short boy with unkempt hair and no jacket, who had fallen asleep sitting cross legged next to me.

"Finn?" I cried, leaping away in surprise. Had he followed me? Was this what he was staring at me for earlier? What did he do while I was unconscious?? Why was he sleeping next to me?

Finn blinked, looking up at me blearily as I had awoken him with my outcry.

"Oh! You're awake!" he replied with a yawn. "Feeling better?"

My eyes darted around suspiciously. We weren't anywhere near the alleyway. So how did I get here?

Finn shifted awkwardly as he seemed to clue in to how this situation looked. My lack of reply seemed to make him even more uncomfortable.

"I found you passed out over there," he explained, scratching his head. "It must have been that 'anemic' thing they keep talking about in *anime*. I've never seen it happen in real life before."

I shot an incredulous look in his direction over his horrible theory. Just how dense could this guy be? But I had to admit, he had effectively stopped my overthinking and panic.

"So, it was all a dream," I sighed in relief.

Finn tilted his head to one side inquisitively, but did not ask any questions. He turned back to the ocean and we both sat there, unmoving, saying nothing for a long time.

Just as I expected, being around him was an incredibly awkward experience.

"Well. Thanks for today," I exclaimed suddenly, deciding to force my escape. "I guess I should head home and get some rest. See you tomorrow Fi-"

"Tanaka…" Finn said in a strangely serious tone as he continued staring out at the water. As much as I had wanted to leave, I now found that my legs refused to move.

"What?"

Finn looked up into my eyes. His usual lethargic glance was now replaced with an intense stare. I shifted nervously. It felt as if he were peering into my very soul, looking for something.

Seeming to have satisfied his search, his expression relaxed back into his usual flat demeanor.

"You mentioned his name when you woke up," Finn said, turning back towards the ocean. "He was the loud blondy in class, right?"

Blondy? I continued to marvel at his unique Japanese. As strangely as he may have said it though, there was no question as to who he was referring to.

"Yeah, that's him all right." I laughed, trying to hide my awkwardness. "Don't tell him I woke up thinking about him. That's the last kind of rumor I need spreading! After all it was…" I paused before continuing, "It was all just a dream."

Finn let out a deep sigh as he picked himself up to his feet. He seemed to be favoring his one arm. I instantly had a flashback to the strange boy in the alleyway who had blocked Tanaka's fist. It had been the same arm.

But that had just been a dream. I thought to myself shaking my head. *There was no point in thinking about it now.*

Once he was on his feet, Finn dusted himself off and then turned to look at me with his hand held out expectantly.

"Umm. Sorry?" I panicked, crossing my arms and turning myself away from him. I wasn't sure why everything this guy did seemed so unnerving.

Finn let out a sigh and then pointed down to my feet.

"My jacket," he replied flatly with his arm held out again.

Looking down I saw that my foot was standing on the sleeve of a folded-up jacket. I must have been lying on it when I was unconscious.

"Ah! I'm so sorry!" I apologized, dusting off the jacket as I picked it up off the ground.

It was covered in mud and grass stains. I must have only made it worse by standing on it. I couldn't believe that I made such a mess of things for him.

Finn shrugged as he took his jacket, throwing it over his shoulder. Without a word he turned around, and casually waved goodbye and walked away.

Maybe he's not so bad after all… I thought as I watched him walk into the distance. *Though he really needs to work on his communication skills.*

It was a great relief to learn the ordeal in the alleyway had all been a dream, but somehow it still felt so real to me.

The stress must be getting to me… I thought, rubbing my eyes as I turned back towards my house.

As I started to walk away, I turned back towards Finn one last time.

It was a dream. I was certain it was. But as Finn walked towards the setting sun, I was almost certain I caught a glimpse of a wolf-like tail wagging behind him.

***

The sight stuck with me for the rest of the night, and the next day in class, I found my eyes constantly drifting back to Finn.

I wasn't certain if he was purposely testing me, or if I was simply going crazy, but I could swear that I saw wolf ears constantly appearing out of the corner of my eye, and then disappearing as soon as I turned towards him.

My frustrations were about to hit a boiling point when I saw a smirk come across his face. He was mocking me, he had to be.

"Hey Mei, did something happen between you and the new guy?" Aki whispered to me at lunch time. "You've been staring at him a lot today."

"I am not usually one to judge another person's love life," Miyori added, "but in all honesty, I would say you can do better."

"What?" I gasped. "No, no! It's not that at all! You're mistaken. Completely wrong!"

Was I really being that obvious? I thought I had only glanced once or twice, but maybe my obsession with this was growing too strong.

Aki put her hands on my shoulders and looked me straight in the eyes with a very concerned expression.

"Mei," she began, staring intently into my eyes. "You aren't one of those *Gaijin Hunters*, are you? Secretly looking for a guy from a foreign country to marry?"

I stared at her blankly, unsure of how to respond to her sincerity, as the grip on my shoulders tightened.

"I will support you no matter what your tastes!" she said, shaking me slightly. "But this world is so big Mei! I'm sure there are guys out there who are better than that! There have to be! Don't be willing to settle so much!"

This was getting out of hand. I needed to end this conversation quickly.

"Come on guys!" I chuckled, "You're just being mean now. I was an inconvenience to him yesterday and was trying to think of a way to thank him. There is nothing betwe-"

Before I could finish my thought, Finn caught is shoulder on some books by the door, knocking them over. Turning around quickly, he managed to catch the stack before they fell to the floor, but his panic allowed me to get a clear view of two large wolf ears and a bushy wolf tail.

All heads turned towards me as I let out a short scream, pointing to Finn as I rose to my feet.

Finn's eyes widened as he put his hand to the wolf ears on his head. There was no way he could deny it now. He awkwardly sidestepped out the door before bursting out into a full sprint but I was not about to let him go.

Nearly tripping over my desk, I charged out the door after Finn, leaving a teary-eyed Aki and confused Miyori behind.

Where did he go? I thought as I ran through the halls. I passed by all manner of students, but no Finn.

Don't tell me he's hiding in the guy's bathroom... I fumed as I had made my way to the top floor of the school. It was about the only place I hadn't checked yet.

The halls were empty as I entered the old section of the school. I debated turning back as I saw the old unused benches coated in undisturbed dust, but as I turned the corner I saw a pair of shoes poking out from behind an old vending machine.

"You... run... surprisingly fast... for such a little guy..." I panted as I approached the vending machine, blocking off Finn's only exit.

Finn glanced around frantically realizing he was trapped. I was not about to let him escape again.

Taking in a deep breath, he looked up at me with a forced smile. It seemed he could get flustered after all...

Now that he was sitting still, I could take a good look at him.

His bushy tail was wrapped around his leg. The furry, pointed ears on top of his head kept twitching, like a dog who knew he had done something wrong but was trying to hide it.

The studded black collar around his neck seemed to be so tight that it was almost choking him. The pendant that hung from it now read the Japanese Kanji for 'fear'.

"So... What is it you wanted to ask me?" Finn asked, nervously avoiding eye contact. "Did I forget something yesterday? I promise I did nothing weird while you were unconscious. I just didn't want to leave you lying in the-"

"Ears…" I interrupted, pointing to the top of his head.

Finn attempted to feign an expression of confusion and innocence, but the wolf ears shot up straight betraying his surprise.

"Ears?" he asked, brushing his hair aside to grab his human ears between his fingers. "Is something wrong with my ears? Do they have something on them? I'm still not used to these vague Japanese senten-"

"Not those," I said, interrupting him yet again. "The wolf ears on top of your head."

Finn's eye twitched slightly, yet he still somehow managed to maintain his composure.

"I'm sorry." He scratched his head with a forced smile. One of the ears cocked off to the side as the other remained straight up. "My Japanese is self-taught, so I am sure there are a lot of expressions I don't understand yet. If you excuse me, I'll just be heading back to cla-"

Finn was still feigning ignorance. I had to make him show his hand but I wasn't sure how. I felt as if my last chance was slipping by as he pushed his way past me.

For a lack of any other ideas, I shot my arm out grabbing him tightly by the tail as he passed me. The fur was coarser than I expected and incredibly thick.

Finn let out a terrified screech as his posture shot straight, but I was not about to let go.

"U-uh M-M-Miyaki w-was it?" he stuttered awkwardly as his knees began to buckle. "W-w-what are you d-d-doing?"

"Oh?" I replied smugly. "What was that? I thought I was just grabbing the air. Or are you going to tell me there is something there after all?"

Finn closed his eyes tightly as I gripped the tail tighter in my hands. He fought remain composed, but a shiver ran up his spine.

"F-f-fine!" he stammered as his legs had almost given out. "Y-y-you were right. I-I apologize! C-c-can you let go now?"

"Only if you tell me what I want to know," I pressed, squeezing the tail again. Finn bent over slightly as his whole body began to shake.

"Okay! Okay!" he cried. "I-I'll tell you anything you want! J-just please let go of that!"

With a satisfied grin, I let go of the tail. Finn took several staggered steps forward before hugging his bushy tail, brushing it gently.

"You shouldn't just grab a guy by the tail, ya know!" he sulked.

He stood there for a while in silence with his back to me, before relaxing his shoulders with a sigh.

"So, you really can see it?" he asked quietly.

I gave a slight nod of acknowledgment.

"But what am I seeing?" I asked. "Yesterday was the first time I had ever seen anything like that in my life!"

Finn cocked his head to one side as if he wasn't expecting to hear that response. Scratching his chin, he pondered something to himself in English.

"Explaining things might be… difficult," he replied.

Frustrated with his evasiveness I reached out for his tail once again. This time, however, his reflexes were faster and he quickly jumped out of the way, hugging his tail tightly.

"MY JAPANESE IS REALLY SIMPLE!" he cried out desperately. "THIS JUNK'S HARD ENOUGH TO EXPLAIN IN ENGLISH! NOW I'VE GOTTA EXPLAIN IT IN JAPANESE AS WELL?!"

My blank stare showed my unwillingness to budge on this issue. Finn's eyes pleaded with me for a minute before he let out a defeated sigh.

"I guess there's no helping it then…" he surrendered. "Come on, I'll see what I can do."

Opening the door beside him, Finn led me into an empty classroom. From the amount of dust lying around, it was safe to assume this classroom hadn't been used in a long time.

What was he going to do in here anyways? I had been so focused on getting answers, I didn't really think things through. Was he looking for a private place to do me in?! Was his secret something I would take with me to the grave?

"How good are you at math?" Finn asked, jarring me from my panic.

"So-so I guess," I replied with a shrug.

I had never been amazing at anything academic, but I wasn't horrible either.

"Well I don't know any academic Japanese." He turned to the chalk board. "So hopefully I can keep this simple for both our sakes!"

Grabbing a piece of chalk, Finn drew a straight line.

"This is the first dimension, or 1D."

He drew three more lines, turning the flat line into a square.

"This is the second dimension, or 2D," he continued.

I nodded, not able to track where he was going with this. Finn however continued his art lesson, drawing several more lines, turning the square into a cube.

"This is the third dimension or 3D… sort of." He replied. "The third dimension is also what we call 'physical space'. It's where matter is. It's where the things we see, smell, hear, taste, and feel are. It includes anything we physically interact with."

I nodded a little slower this time. This lesson had just taken a rather sharp spike in complexity, but I was still able to follow... sort of.

"These are most of the dimensions anyone ever talks about," Finn continued. "These are the only dimensions most people can observe."

Finn looked straight into my eyes and the corner of his mouth curled up into a smile.

"But what if there were dimensions beyond this?" he explained.

Turning back to the board he drew a smaller cube inside the first which appeared to be both inside and outside the cube.

I turned back to him with a confused expression. He seemed disappointed, yet not surprised at my lack of understanding.

Reaching into his pocket, Finn pulled out a cell phone and held it out to face me.

"Do you text your friends often?" he asked, opening a messaging app.

I nodded. Who didn't text their friends in this day and age?

Finn smiled as he continued fiddling with his phone

"Have you ever had it where you knew what your friends were thinking, even though you couldn't see them or hear their voice? Or times where you felt physically hurt, or comforted by what someone said, even though it's really just words on a screen?"

My patience was wearing thin. His explanation seemed to be raising more questions than answers.

"Okay, that's true, but what are you getting at?" I asked, crossing my arms. "What does geometry and technology have to do with what I've been seeing?"

Finn rubbed his forehead as he tried to think of a simpler way to explain.

"What if I told you that our personalities and emotions existed separately from, but connected to, our physical bodies?" he asked, while tugging on the ear on top of his head.

"What if I told you that the fourth dimension was where the REAL us existed? Where who a person truly is, and what they are feeling, can be observed?"

Pointing back to the picture on the chalk board he continued, "The same way a 3D object can be observed in the 2D world, yet can never fit entirely in it, our fourth-dimension selves bleed through into our third-dimension selves. It comes through in our actions, expressions, even the chemicals our bodies produce, but you can never see all there is to a person by only looking at their body. There is so much more to people than can be confined to the physical dimension."

I examined Finn's face, trying to determine if he was being serious, or just leading me on. You could observe someone's emotions and personalities? It seemed crazy!

As my eyes drifted, I watched Finn's bushy tail wagging behind him.

It seemed crazy… but I couldn't deny what I was seeing.

"Let's say I believe you," I said slowly. "How does this explain your having wolf ears and a tail?"

Finn let out another sigh as he considered his words.

"I said that our five senses detect physical objects in the third dimension," he explained. "Normally people can only use those senses, and because of that they can only observe what they see in the third dimension. They form opinions about people based on what they see them do. They build relationships with people slowly by gathering experiences with them. It's really a depressing way to live when you think about it."

Finn pointed to the ears on top of his head.

"But sometimes people develop new senses. Senses capable of observing the fourth dimension.

Apparently, these senses vary slightly between individuals. You keep talking about seeing things… for me it is more of a cross between hearing and feeling pressures. I know what exists, and what it means, but I can't see the level of detail you say you can. I am a little envious, actually."

Absentmindedly I rubbed my eyes. They didn't feel any different, but something about me had changed. Had the shock from yesterday knocked something loose?

Taking a deep breath, I turned to Finn.

"The incident in the alleyway last night. I didn't dream that, did I…? Something really did happen to Tanaka, didn't it?"

Finn's smile disappeared.

"Tanaka…" he sighed, rubbing his head again.

Lifting his arm, Finn tensed his hand. His fingers changed, turning into the red clawed hand I had seen the other day.

"As we grow, we make choices that change us." He looked away from me and down at his hand. "What do you want to live for in life? What do you hope for? What are you afraid of? What do you anticipate? What do you love? What do you hate? Which of those will you focus on?

Each person will change. Even if you don't address the tough questions in life, those tough questions will still be shaping you."

Finn leaned against the window, watching as the various students moved around in the courtyard below.

"As we change, our fourth-dimension form begins to take shape. Both the ways we interact with others, and the ways others interact with us are reflected in that form."

He took a deep breath.

"Sometimes we let one influence in our life take too much control." He glanced at me. "Maybe you feel betrayed by someone and you can't let it go. Maybe you feel weak and powerless, and your fears are taking over. Maybe there's an incident from your childhood you can't come to accept, and so you try to bury it, and deny that it ever happened."

Finn paused again.

"When one influence takes control, your fourth-dimension form will begin to warp. It will grow in ways you are unable to control as that single influence monopolizes your entire being. Then, when it has grown large enough, you lose yourself completely, and turn into what this world calls a 'monster.' Unable to think or be reasoned with. Every action is simply you reacting to your now single driving force."

"Then Tanaka…" I gasped. I couldn't accept what I was hearing. I had never really liked Tanaka, but as I was reminded of my attempts to reason with that monster in the alleyway, I suddenly felt a squeezing pain within my heart.

For a while, Finn didn't say anything, but he continued looking out the window.

"Tanaka, it seems, had grown up in a family with a lot of bitterness," he said at last. "They blamed the government, the people around them, the elderly, the youth, and they especially blamed foreigners for all that was wrong in the world. They blamed everyone but themselves, and felt completely powerless to stop it."

Finn clenched his fists and continued to stare out the window, but his eyes were distant.

"Growing up he was taught to blame all the world's problems on those around him. He was constantly told how everyone who thought otherwise were idiots. Warned that people would try to manipulate him to believe otherwise.

Growing up believing there was no one he could trust but himself, his pride and bitterness began to consume him.

What was the point of listening to people when they were just mindlessly following others? How could he make connections with people who couldn't see what, to him, was so obvious? The more these thoughts took over, the more his fourth-dimension form warped and twisted.

He no longer had eyes to see those around him, or ears to hear what others said… He wanted the world to come to his side and see what he could see, but was afraid of becoming what the world already was.

On the outside, he was a giant monster of pride, built for nothing but blind violence and anger. But on the inside, he was a tormented soul, shackled by fear to a world of loneliness."

There was a clattering of tables as my legs gave out and I attempted to catch myself.

"No…" I cried. "So now he's…"

Finn turned away from the window and panicked as he saw me.

"Whoa, whoa, whoa!" he cried, running to my side. "Don't give up yet! Like I said, when someone turns into a monster, they are beyond a *normal* person's ability to help them."

Finn put a hand on my shoulder and I looked up to see him staring me straight in the eyes with a slight smile.

"But *we* are not normal people, are we?" he replied.

"Then Tanaka's all right?" I asked.

Finn nodded with a smile.

"He's taking a few days to rethink some things, but he should be back soon."

"How did you do it?" I asked, wiping a tear away.

Finn raised his hand and the claws appeared once again.

"Remember when you grabbed my tail?" he replied, and stood up.

I nodded as he instinctively pulled his tail away from me.

"With practice, someone who can observe the fourth dimension can learn to interact with it.

Your fourth-dimension form is connected, but not bound to your physical body. What looks like a simple conversation to the casual onlooker is an epic battle of life and death to us. A struggle between two fourth dimensional forms to see which will survive. It's basically learning how to fight feelings with feelings."

"Fight feelings with feelings?" I repeated, sounding apprehensive. "How is that supposed to work?"

"People become monsters because they let one influence take over their entire being," Finn explained. "We have the ability to observe the root of the problem. We see peoples' weaknesses, but also their strengths. Essentially, we fight to weaken the hold that influence has on a person, while encouraging their own strengths to fight back.

You have to be careful though. As you connect with their fourth-dimension self, they connect with yours. The same way you are trying to weaken that one influence, that one influence will be lashing out desperately and trying to destroy you in order to survive.

"So, in Tanaka's case?" I asked wearily. We had officially gone over my head.

Finn leaned back and thought for a moment.

"People like Tanaka are actually pretty common where I come from." He continued, "Whether by hating others, or hating those who hate others… bitterness is a very nasty influence to deal with. It is like a ball of barbed hooks. The tighter you hold onto it, the more it hurts you, but the less you feel like you can ever let it go."

"So how do you remove it?" I asked.

"Painfully." Finn replied.

"First you need to rip out the pride. Pride is found at the source of most problems. Confidence builds us up, but pride destroys us. It blinds us to our weaknesses by using the fear of being wrong or weak.

The only way to remove it is by realizing that they *are* in fact weak, limited, klutzy — but proving that there is strength in accepting your weakness and pushing forward through it."

I nodded, as he continued.

"Once pride is dealt with, you face bitterness. You cannot beat hate with hate. If you try to, your opponent's hate will only feel justified and grow stronger.

You have to endure it. You have to stand strong. You have to meet hate with love, and show that all the misconceptions they hold about you are wrong."

Finn shook his head. "People aren't dumb. We ignore what we don't want to see out of pride and fear, but when reality differs enough from what we believe, we owe it to ourselves to question it.

And that is where Tanaka is now. Questioning things. Rethinking what he knows and doesn't know. Reshaping his fourth-dimension form into what he wants to be."

The bell rang signaling the end of lunch. Finn looked at me as if to ask, "Is that good enough?" to which I let out a long sigh.

"I guess that will do for now," I mumbled, though I felt like I had raised even more questions than I had gained answers for.

We left the room together and began to walk back to class.

"Hey Finn?" I asked as we made our way back to the new part of the school.

Finn looked at me, awaiting my question.

"Why did you come to Japan?"

Finn scratched his head as he considered my question.

"Growing up, I never had anyone around to explain why I could notice the things I did." He explained looking at his clawed hand. "If a guy can see stuff no one else can, he'll be a genius when others can see it too. Until then he's just considered nuts."

"It sounds rough," I empathized.

Finn nodded.

"I would have gone crazy, I think," he agreed, "but then I found a book written by a guy named Minasaki Tatsuya."

"Minasaki Tatsuya?" I inquired. I couldn't think of any famous authors with that name.

"It was from his book that I managed to piece together the theory I told you." Finn smiled. "It was thanks to him that I realized I wasn't crazy or alone in this world."

"Alone?" I was surprised. "Aren't there others like us out there?"

Finn let out a defeated laugh.

"You're the first I've ever met." He sighed. He seemed very lonely, but also a little thankful. Like a lost child who finally had a stranger check in on him.

"I see." I looked at my shoes. "So, you came to Japan because of this author?"

Finn gave an odd smirk as he walked.

"It seems silly I guess. But I thought maybe if I could meet him, I could meet other people who understood this better than me. I want to learn, and understand."

We didn't say anything else on the way back to class, but there were a lot of thoughts running through my head as I reached for the door.

CHAPTER THREE

Swords and Armor

Any hopes I had of returning to my normal life were lost the moment I walked through the classroom door.

Everyone looked... different. Some had large ears, others extra arms, fur, scales, feathers, or wrinkles. There were so many different shapes and forms.

There were far too many sights to take in at once, and each person I saw filled my mind with numerous thoughts and emotions. It was as if my mind was being flooded with textbook's worth of information for every face I looked at.

"Are you all right, Mei?" Aki whispered to me during class as I buried my head in my arms on my desk.

"You were acting weird at lunch and now you seem so tired. You aren't getting sick, are you?"

I looked up at Aki. Her usual hair barrettes now sat at the base of a pair of long, white rabbit-like ears. It seemed fitting for such a cute and bouncy individual. Her cheeks seemed a little rosier, and her eyes seemed even wider than usual. There seemed to be something moving around her.

As I looked closer, I noticed wires which were as thin as fishing line seemed to glint in the light around her. I tried to focus, but my head began aching again before I could get a good look at them.

"I'm all right Aki," I replied, lowering my head again. "I just had to run a bit during lunch and now I'm feeling pretty worn out."

"If you say so…" Aki replied, still sounding worried.

I'm sorry Aki. I thought. *I don't want to lie to you, but I don't think I could explain this if I tried.*

The day dragged on for what felt like an eternity. I couldn't look at anyone for more than a few seconds without getting sick, and my head kept getting hit with waves of pain.

As my mind was flooded with information, my heart was being flooded with emotions. Happiness, heartbreak, fear, disgust, anger, excitement. It was too much to handle at such a rapid pace.

I felt like I was going to die. Tears began to form in my eyes, but somehow, I managed to hang on until the final bell rang.

Aki and Miyori didn't say much as they headed off to their club activities. Aki lent me her water bottle telling me to stay hydrated, and Miyori advised I go home to get some rest. They sounded like their usual cheery selves, but I felt a painful gripping at my heart from their worry and concern.

Once they had left, I took a deep breath and made my way straight to a certain shaggy head who was sitting casually at his desk reading a book.

"Mei?" Finn jumped to attention as I slapped my hands down in front of him. I was breathing heavily as I tried to think through the throbbing pain in my head.

"How do you turn it off?!" I growled through gritted teeth.

"Turn it off?" he pondered staring up at me. "Oh! You mean what we were talking about earlier?"

The world spun as I nodded.

"You can't," he stated, turning back to his book.

"Wait… what?" I gasped. "But… You've got to be able to turn it off! How else can you function? I can't even look at anyone! My brain feels like it wants to explode!"

"Yeah, I know." Finn replied with a chuckle. "It's really a pain isn't it?"

I rubbed my forehead, but the pain refused to retreat.

"You mean you deal with this 24/7?" I asked.

"How else do you think my eyes got to be like this?" Finn replied, pointing to the dark bags under his eyes.

Dejected, I fell back against the desk behind me.

"No way…" I cried. "I can't live like this… I don't want this!"

Finn looked up from his book again. His expression softened as he saw the exhaustion in my face.

"How do you turn off seeing?" he asked. "How do you turn off your sense of smell or your ability to hear?

This isn't a super power. It's just a sense. And it's a sense you haven't used up until now.

The same way you had to learn how to get used to bright lights, loud noises, and strong smells, you'll have to learn to adapt to strong personalities, deep wounds, and big egos as well. Though there are a few tricks that make things easier."

"Tricks?" I asked, turning back towards him.

"Hmm, well let's see," Finn pondered. "Like, 'avoid looking people straight in the eye as much as possible'."

Finn must have become accustomed to seeing me confused as he continued his explanation without further prompting.

"Eyes are like windows to the soul. As you get used to your abilities you'll come to find that you can gather information from just about anything. Reading their writing, hearing their voice, sheesh, I've even gained information from seeing peoples' hands or feet before! But *nothing* gives you more insight into a person's heart than looking straight into their eyes. They're like a deep pit of thoughts and emotions that draw you in and go on forever."

"So, avoiding eye contact will keep my head from getting overwhelmed?" I asked.

"Well, it should make it easier at least." He pondered, "Though it won't help your social life any I'm afraid."

Groaning again I buried my head in my hands. How was I going to keep my head from exploding until I could adapt?

Finn was about to add something, when a new voice interrupted.

"Excuse me. Finn Coller, wasn't it?" the strong male voice called out from behind me.

I turned around to see Oga Souma, the male class rep. At least, the voice sounded like Oga's…

Normally Oga was a tall, well-dressed guy with neatly parted hair wearing glasses. He was a stickler for rules and fairness, which would normally make him unbearable, but earnestness and sincerity had earned him his place in class.

What I saw standing before me now however, was a massive suit of armor, carrying a sword so large it looked like it had come from a *manga*.

The word 'Justice' was written in large kanji across the chest plate of the armor, and the giant sword had the kanji 'Duty' written in a similar manner.

Even though I couldn't see Oga's face, I felt an uneasiness about him, as if he were bracing himself, ready to attack at any given moment.

"Oga!" I called out, trying to intercept, but Finn raised his hand to stop me.

"Yep. I'm Finn alright." Finn seemed to be bracing himself as well. "Is something the matter?"

"Finn Coller…" Oga replied adjusting his posture. "I am sorry I was unable to welcome you to class yesterday as I was absent at the time of your arrival. That being said, there is something I feel it is my duty as class rep to discuss with you."

Oga's giant suit of armor lifted the massive sword clumsily above his head, barely able to maintain his balance.

"There have been several concerns raised against you by various members of the class. From your sloppy dress, to your lackluster responses. Now there is even a rumor about you having done something to the currently absent Tanaka Shoma, and I see you causing grief to a female member of our class!"

I started to shake my head to deny the accusation, but the look Finn sent my way stopped me.

Oga continued, beginning to swing the blade as he spoke. "I have been sent to make you aware of the rules and expectations of a student of our school, in order for us to maintain a safe and friendly environment to learn and grow to the best of our abilities!"

The heavy blade made its way rapidly towards Finn's shoulder, however, he refused to budge.

At first, I felt like crying out for Oga to stop, but then I remembered how Finn had managed to stop Tanaka's attack the other day with one hand.

He'll be fine. I thought to myself. *After all, no one would simply let someone hurt the-*

My thoughts were cut short as the sword hit Finn straight in the chest, causing him to grip at his heart in pain.

"Finn!" I cried out, rushing up beside him.

"What are you doing!?" I whispered. "Didn't you see that coming towards you? Why didn't you stop that sword like what you did yesterday?!"

"This isn't the same as yesterday." Finn raised a finger to my lips and then gestured at Oga.

"Look at him. That armor and sword aren't part of his normal fourth dimension form. They're things he willed onto himself. He's not attacking me because he wants to. He built that armor and weapon out of the duty he feels towards his role. It's his attempt to strengthen the areas he feels weak in.

Even if he's wrong about what I've done, I can't feel malice against a guy who's earnestly trying to take on his own weakness like that."

"So what?" I protested. "You're just going to sit there and let him hurt you because his heart's in the right place?!"

"Others can't see this world," Finn reminded me. "If my taking a few hits means he'll be strong enough to help others in the future, I'll just have to grin and bear it. It would be immature of me to risk hurting him just for the sake of my feelings."

As I stepped back, I saw Finn still clenching at his chest as Oga struggled to raise the massive sword for another strike. Unlike Tanaka who flung his giant fists so easily, it seemed like the sword was truly difficult for Oga to use. I couldn't stand by to watch these two hurt themselves any longer.

"What was it you said about pride making you feel like you can only trust yourself?" I asked flatly.

Finn's eyes widened as I turned back to Oga.

"Oga!" I shouted. "You're wrong!"

A loud popping sound was heard as cracks began to form in Oga's armor. His grip on his sword seemed to falter.

"What?" he asked in surprise. "Weren't you being bothered by this classmate just now?"

"Miyaki!" Finn whispered. "What are you doing? I'm fine! Don't destroy the confidence he's worked so hard to build up! This class will need him!"

Finn's pleading sounded earnest, but as I saw the gash in his chest, I chose to ignore it.

"I was upset about something else," I continued. "Finn saw me upset and tried to encourage me."

Another popping sound was heard as the armor cracked further revealing Oga's worried face through a hole in the helmet. I still wasn't done.

"And as for Tanaka, I saw him yesterday too." I shook my head for emphasis. "He was being violent and not himself. Finn checked in on him to see if he was all right, but that was it!"

A sound like breaking glass could be heard as Oga's armor shattered and the pieces fell to the ground and disappeared.

"So, I was… scolding an innocent man…" Oga gasped. His eyes seemed distant as he realized what he had done.

Oga turned to me, Finn, then back to the ground as he attempted to piece everything together. Turning back to Finn, he bowed furiously before him.

"I AM SINCERELY SORRY FOR MY IMPUDENCE!" he cried out. "It was wrong of me to jump to conclusions! I am truly ashamed of my actions and the pain I brought to you! I hope you will not think less of me for it!"

After bowing, Oga left the classroom in a hurry, his cheeks were flushed with embarrassment. I turned to see Finn kneeling on the ground, wide-eyed.

"Why did you do that…" he asked almost half to himself. "What if you damaged him… What if this plants an influence that destroys him? What if he turns into a mo-"

The loud sound of my hand slapping against his cheek rang out in the classroom stopping his rambling.

He sat there, simply stunned for a second, before gingerly touching the tender red spot on his face.

"Idiot!" I scolded as he continued his vacant stare. "If you're so scared about other people and what damage bad experiences will do to them, why aren't you afraid for yourself!?"

Finn tried to speak, but then stopped as he saw the sincerity in my eyes.

"Have faith in people, Finn," I exclaimed. "We're all a lot stronger than you think!"

Finn's arms drooped to his sides as he fell back in his chair, deep in thought.

Looking closer at him, I could see the wound across his chest where Oga's sword had hit him.

"Is that as bad as it looks?" I asked.

If it had been a physical wound, his heart would have nearly been pierced, but since it was his fourth dimensional self, no blood poured from it. The gaping wound seemed to lead to a black swirling void of emptiness.

Finn rubbed the wound gingerly. "The price we pay for sensitivity," he mumbled.

"It's great to be able to observe the fourth dimension, and it makes us much more aware of the feelings of those around us. The downside though, as I'm sure you've noticed, is that it also makes us a lot more susceptible to the feelings of others as well."

Finn let out a heavy sigh then leapt back to his feet.

"Well!" he exclaimed clapping his hands. "Wounds can disappear over time if we let them! So long as I don't obsess over how he hurt me, and accept that he meant well despite the result, no bitterness should take root in this wound and it should heal... mostly."

I let out a sigh as I leaned against the wall, feeling exhausted.

"This isn't going to be easy, is it..." I mumbled, looking down at my hands.

Finn smiled and placed his hand on my head.

"It's a rough life," he admitted, "but I think the world needs people like us. I like to think we were made this way for a reason. I think as you get used to your abilities you'll start to see what I mean."

I looked up at him as he smiled sweetly at me.

He wasn't a bad guy. He was trying his best to comfort me in the way he wished someone had been there to comfort him growing up. In a way I really appreciated it... but seriously?

"Umm Finn..." I asked. "What is with this hand?"

Finn let out a panicked yelp and staggered back a few feet.

"I'm so sorry!" he apologized. "I thought it was a Japanese thing to do when someone was upset! I totally overstepped my bounds! I can't believe that. I am so sorry! I'll never do it again. Please don't hate me!"

Watching Finn so flustered, I couldn't help but burst out laughing.

"Did you study anything other than *anime* to learn about Japan?" I asked after I caught my breath.

He was so observant in some ways, yet so oblivious in others. I didn't have any idea what would be lying ahead for me, but at least I had someone who already had some experience, so I was already ahead of what some people would deal with.

Finn looked at me inquisitively as I reached out my hand towards him.

"This is what they do where you're from isn't it?" I asked.

Finn cautiously returned my gesture as I gave him a sturdy handshake.

"You can call me Mei," I said with a smile. "It's a pleasure to be working with you, Finn!"

CHAPTER FOUR

Tangled Vines

"Hey, did you hear about the new kid in 1D?" a boy in Class 1B asked his friend while sitting on his desk.

"You mean the *gaijin*?" another replied.

A blond head of hair perked up as the conversation went on.

"Apparently he was a huge let down," the second continued. "At least us guys have nothing to worry about from him."

The head lowered again.

"But I've heard he did win over one girl," the first added.

The blond hair rose yet again.

"Miyaki Mei, wasn't it?" the other boy said. "I hear they've been seen together alone a lot recently. Man, I guess being from another country really does give you an advantage in love. Maybe I should try out for a foreign exchange program!"

A chair screeched across the ground as a blond-haired girl rose ceremoniously to her feet.

She was Tohka Chika, a school idol. Beloved by the boys, and scorned by the girls — not that it ever seemed to bother her.

"Class 1D," Tohka mused as she walked out of her classroom door. "Perhaps I should give this *gaijin* my own style of warm welcome."

***

Whispers spread throughout Class 1D as Tanaka entered the classroom.

It had been two weeks since he had marched out of class and students had begun to talk. There were rumors of Finn having 'dealt' with him in a North American fashion. It had grown to the point of people asking if Finn had mafia ties, and if he had only come to Japan to avoid a gang war.

Finn took the rumors in his usual lackluster stride. It would be difficult for the casual onlooker to tell if he was oblivious, or a masochist, but with my eyes it was getting easier to notice the various wounds he had been covering up.

As for myself, I was finally starting to adjust to my new life. The headaches were fewer and farther between, and I had finally reached a point where Finn suggested I should start trying to focus on people one at a time.

Since he had suggested I start with people I was already familiar with, I had spent the last hour of class focusing on Aki while she sat beside me.

I had finally gotten used to her bunny-like ears, which seemed to suit her attentive, innocent, energetic nature, and the larger eyes seemed to simply add to her natural cuteness. But the numerous wires that seemed to tug on her from all directions had me worried.

"Anxiety." Finn had told me when I asked him during lunch. "A strong feeling of duty and desire to not let anyone down can quickly overwhelm you."

"It's an easy trap to fall into. You care about the people around you. You're afraid to let them down. You're afraid of messing up, being left alone, or being looked down on. All it takes is one or two well-meaning people who try to push you forward, and suddenly you're trying to live up to expectations you could never fulfill.

You want to please everyone. You don't want to let anyone down. You can't ask for help or say no to anyone because doing so would prove you are weak and that would turn them against you. Meanwhile as you take everything upon yourself, you begin to get overwhelmed by every possibility, as if every potential disaster rests on your shoulders alone.

You can't rest without feeling like you're letting someone down. You can't focus on one person without feeling you're abandoning everyone else. You can't ask for help without feeling like you'll lose your value to others. It's like winding a spring tighter and tighter until the day comes when it finally snaps. It's a deadly influencer."

When Aki spoke with other people she had always been so peppy and energetic. She was always smiling and seemed so confident. It was hard to believe she had been suffering so much all this time.

She never stayed in one place for long, and was always taking on new jobs or talking to new people. I had always ascribed that to her short attention span more than anything else.

But every so often, when she thought no one else was watching, her true feelings started to show

The long ears on Aki's head began to droop as her mind seemed to wander from class, and the wires tightened. Occasionally one would twitch, tugging her in one direction or another. Her lip began to tremble as her eyes began to slowly fall shut.

"Hey Aki, is everything all right?" I asked, pulling her from her trance. Her ears shot straight up, and the wires seemed to relax a little.

Aki seemed taken aback by my question. She searched my eyes for a moment, looking both worried and thankful. The wires tightened again as she put on her usual sunny expression.

"Silly Mei!" she smiled. "There's no need for you to be worrying about me! I'm fine. I'm more worried about you. You've seemed so worn out recently!"

Before, I would have been relieved by this answer. I would have believed that she was still her happy, cheerful self. But as I looked at her now, her bright eyes and smile looked like a well-worn mask. Though she acted so energetic, her body looked ready to collapse. The numerous wires protruding from her were the only thing left holding her up.

Aki's bunny ears began to twitch awkwardly as my concerned expression remained unchanged.

"You don't have to carry everything by yourself." I put a hand on her shoulder. "You don't need to keep up appearances with me. I'm here for you through thick and thin."

Aki's eyes widened as she looked at me. It was like the mask she was wearing was beginning to crack. She was about to speak up when the door to the classroom burst open.

"Everyone! Please excuse me!" an annoyingly feminine voice called out sounding very unapologetic.

Every boy stood up and gasped as a girl with shoulder length blond hair, pale skin and blue eyes walked into the class.

Who is that? I thought as she swayed into class, running her fingers through her hair with a confident smile.

My attention was brought back to Aki, who had stood up from her seat, staring down at her desk with a scowl on her face.

"I'm sorry Mei," she muttered, looking away. "I… have to go to track."

I called out after her, but it was too late. Aki ran out the door as the girl who had just entered glanced after her with a victorious smirk.

Seriously. Who is this girl?! I was starting to get annoyed as I watched her survey the class. As if in reply to my question, the boys began to whisper to one another.

"It's her! It's her!" one boy whispered excitedly.

"Tohka Chika? The idol from 1B?? What is she doing here!?" another boy gasped.

"She is such a refreshing breeze of fresh air." A third boy sighed. "Why can't she be in our class?"

"Because she's too smart for us Class D idiots!" the first boy answered.

The girls weren't saying anything, but had all huddled into groups and were staring daggers towards Tohka. It didn't take any stretch of imagination to understand why.

Turning towards Tohka, I decided to get a better look at her.

Blond hair, blue eyes, pale skin. She seemed to be only half Japanese?

She had a nice figure, and her clothing seemed to be meticulously adjusted in all the right places to better show that fact off. Her makeup was prominent but not overwhelming, her complexion was without blemish, and her skirt seemed to be shortened to show off the full length of her long legs. Just how much effort did this girl put into her look?

Catching movement from the corner of my eye, I noticed what looked like thorny vines growing out from her body and traveling along the floor. They worked their way around the numerous chairs and desks, each one making their way to a different guy. They wrapped themselves around each one, working their way up their bodies, the thorns digging into their flesh. The ends of the vines stopped at their hearts where they pierced their way into their chests.

Even Tanaka, who was doing his best to appear disinterested, was bound tightly by the spiky thorns.

The only boy who seemed unaffected was Finn. He sat at his desk, staring out the window in his usual oblivious manner.

Tohka scanned the room, ignoring both the lustful stares and vicious glares she was receiving. When she caught sight of Finn, the corner of her mouth turned up into a malicious smirk and she walked sensually to his desk.

"Well hello there!" she called out cheerfully, leaning low across Finn's desk. "You must be the new student I've heard so much about!"

Finn turned away from the window and raised an eyebrow as he saw the beautiful face invading his personal bubble.

"Umm... Yo." He replied in his usual detached manner, giving a slight wave of his hand.

Like a true socializing expert, Tohka giggled at Finn's response.

"What's with that halfhearted greeting?" she smiled, pulling up a chair and sitting down across from him. "Come on now, I don't bite!"

As Tohka reached out her hand towards Finn, a thorny vine began to slither over his shoulder. Finn's ear twitched as the vine's thorns scratched against his neck, but otherwise he didn't react.

"This is how you introduce yourself to people where you're from isn't it?" Tohka asked shyly. "Am I doing it right? I know how scary it can be to live in another country with all new languages and customs. I want you to feel comfortable with me."

Finn let out a subtle sigh as he stretched out his hand towards Tohka's.

No sooner had he reached out his hand, then the vine over his shoulder shot across his chest.

Instead of the usual one-handed handshake like I had given him earlier, Tohka grabbed Finn's hand in both of her own while she leaned in even closer.

The vine curled back around Finn's back where the end began to branch out into numerous other vines, working their way around his neck, chest, and arms.

"Believe it or not, my mother is from overseas as well." Her expression said that she sympathized with Finn, but my eyes told me otherwise. "I'm sure it's not the same as what you are going through, but I know how hard it can be to stand out in a school like this. Why, even my hair and eye colour seems to draw everyone's stares!"

Tohka looked over her shoulder, still holding firmly onto Finn's hand. She smirked as all the boys who had been staring at Finn enviously, averted their eyes in shame.

As she turned back towards Finn, her triumphant expression seamlessly returned to a face of care and concern.

"I want to make sure your time at this school will be full of wonderful memories! I want you to make sure your time in Japan holds some wonderful memories for you, and…"

Tohka paused slightly while averting her eyes. Her grip on Finn's hand tightened as her face began to blush slightly. This girl was truly an artist.

"I… think it would be really nice if I could have someone to talk to about non-Japanese things." She added quietly, "If you would allow me to be so selfish."

As Tohka's face grew redder, the branching vines around Finn's body began to position themselves above his heart.

It was so obvious she was leading him on. Any other guy would be completely wrapped around her little finger by now

But this is Finn. She has no idea what she's in for! I thought with a smirk.

"Sure thing," Finn replied while pulling his hand out of the blonde's grip. "I'd be glad to help."

I nearly fell out of my seat.

Was he actually accepting her offer? But that was impossible. He had to realize what was going on by now. Her treacherous vines were everywhere. How could he not see —

Oh wait… that's right. I'd just had a horrific realization.

Finn had already told me that he couldn't 'see' the fourth dimension. It was some sort of strange sense specific to me. Did that mean he couldn't tell what was happening right now? I mean sure he was usually great at reading people, but he could also be surprisingly dense from time to time.

"Really?!" Tohka cried out, leaping forward, and grabbing Finn's retreating hand once again.

The vines had tightened around his arms and neck. The branches hovering above his heart pulled slightly preparing to strike.

Finn's eyes turned to the window for a moment. Was he feeling bashful?

I had no time to consider this however, as Tohka took the opportunity to shoot me a triumphant glance.

Wait... What on earth was that?? I stared as Tohka smirked straight at me.

I looked around and there was clearly no one else that glance could have been aimed at. Did Tohka hold something against me? I had never met her before. Was I supposed to feel jealous that she getting so close to Finn? But why would I do that?

Wait... she didn't think I liked him, did she?

I looked up at Finn. He was sitting there in his usual slouched posture, his clothes wrinkled and his hair a complete mess.

No, not even she could be that wrong. I thought, shaking my head.

The boys around the classroom were all glaring at Finn. The vines which pierced their hearts were slowly being torn out. Each thorn tore away at their flesh as the vine was removed. I could barely stand to watch, it looked so painful.

Finn and Tohka on the other hand seemed to be in a world all their own.

"I'm so glad," Tohka cried. "Maybe we can meet for lunch on Saturday!"

"Sure. Sounds fine." Finn seemed to have accepted that he was never going to get his hand back again as he leaned back in his chair.

Tohka's expression changed slightly as the vines hovering over Finn's heart wove together, forming into a sharp point.

"I guess I should be careful," she added with a wink. "I have heard that *gaijin* are real heart stealers!"

I felt like the air in the room thinned out as all the boys in the room swallowed at once.

The girls who had been silent began whispering again, looking both disgusted and shocked. Even if she had a reputation of winning over every guy she met, was she willing to go as low as Finn?

How could Tohka handle having this much negative attention sent her way? As her eyes roved the room she looked like she could hardly contain her ecstasy. Was she enjoying this?

Looking towards Finn, I tried to make him hear my thoughts by willpower alone.

Come on Finn. Don't listen to her! I thought. *She's obvious! She is so, so obvious! Even you can do better than this!*

As I stared intently at Finn, I noticed the corner of his mouth twitched as his tail began to wag.

"Oh, I wouldn't worry about that," he said casually. "After all, you could do much better than someone like me, right?"

"Pardon?" Tohka asked, letting go of Finn's hands. She seemed taken aback by the thought that someone would push away from her. The rest of the class stared in shock.

This time Finn was the one to lean forward.

Staring intently into her eyes. Tohka's face began to turn red again, though this time involuntarily. For the first time since she had entered the classroom, she was on the defense.

"Hmm…" Finn continued staring deep into Tohka's eyes, unfazed by her discomfort.

"I would say you want a guy who will pay attention to you. One who sees the real you and loves it. Not just Tohka the school idol, but Tohka the lonely girl who wants someone to see her as more than just a pretty face.

I think you want someone who isn't afraid to take charge from time to time, yet respects your opinion enough to hear you out. You don't want a guy who follows you. You want a guy who will walk with you. But a guy like me would probably seem too boring for an exciting girl like yourself!"

Tohka stood to her feet while Finn raised the other hand that he had hidden behind his back.

The clawed hand gripped tightly onto the main vine that had wrapped around him. With a slight squeeze, the vines withered away as if they had caught on fire.

"I've gotta stop by the bathroom now, but I'm totally up for hanging out this weekend." He rose from his chair, brushing the remaining vines off in one swift movement. "Let me know when you want to meet up."

Tohka fell back to her chair, speechless as Finn stopped a few feet away.

"By the way," he added, "This might be more than I should say, but I think you should show that real you more often. I think she's a much more interesting person to talk to!"

All the vines throughout the class seemed to dry up and dissolve at once as Finn walked casually out.

Tohka sat in silence, unsure what had just happened.

Eventually she got up and left the classroom without a word, staring intently down at the hand she had originally extended to Finn.

As soon as she left the classroom, the other students all gathered in groups to discuss what had happened.

The boys seemed ready to gang up on Finn for daring to say such offensive things to their precious idol, while the girls seemed rather smug about the *gaijin* being good for something after all.

Eventually, they all split up and went their separate ways to go home or to their clubs. It wouldn't take long though for rumors of this incident to spread throughout the school.

Eventually I was the only one left in class, but I wasn't about to leave just yet.

I waited for about ten minutes until the classroom door opened again.

"So, when did you catch on?" I asked as Finn reentered the classroom.

Finn shrugged as he walked to his desk and picked up his bag.

"The moment she looked at me I guess." He shrugged. "Stuff like that is usually pretty easy for me to catch."

"Was it the vines?" I asked as I grabbed my bag as well.

"Is that what they were?" Finn asked. "I had noticed she seemed to be tied to a lot of people, but as I said before, I can't 'see' this stuff, just sense it."

"So you could tell from the multiple connections?" I prodded further.

Finn shook his head.

"That was a hint for sure." He admitted, "But it was far more obvious than that."

Standing up straight, Finn puffed out his chest and smiled.

"Whenever a girl tries to flirt with a guy like me, it can only ever mean that she's trying to get something from him!"

I stared at Finn blankly as he smiled with pride. I sighed and turned back towards the door.

"Don't say such depressing things so proudly." I muttered, as I walked out to head home. I couldn't believe I had just waited for so long to hear such a pathetic explanation.

Finn cocked his head to one side as I left the classroom. He was a klutz and a fool, but there were times when he could almost be impressive, in his own strange little way.

CHAPTER FIVE

Allies and Burdens

As the weeks passed by, I continued to adapt to my life with this new perspective.

Being able to see people's feelings and personalities didn't help my social life very much. In fact, it made it a lot harder to be social at all.

Being around people was exhausting. Being in crowded places often made both my head and heart ache as all the feelings and life stories would pour into my head.

That isn't to say there were no benefits. While I couldn't hang out with as many people as I could before, I found the quality of my relationships rose dramatically.

People had always been a mystery to me. The people who were nice to me I liked. The people who hurt me I didn't. I had always taken the actions of others personally. Those who were good to me were good people who liked me. Those who weren't were bad people who hated me.

I thought people were either good or evil. And likewise, people were the source of all evil or good in the world... but now I was beginning to see the world was a far more complicated place.

People were not good or evil themselves, but they were capable of actions for good or evil purposes, which had results that were good or evil separate from their intentions.

Sometimes people would hurt others completely by accident, but more commonly it was due to the choices they had made, and what they had let become a dominant influence in their lives.

Often our greatest strength could end up becoming our greatest weakness. Often the things we hated the most in others, were things we struggled with ourselves.

Someone who was outgoing and confident could quickly become oblivious to the feelings of others and as a result end up hurting their friends.

Someone who was humble and patient could become self-degrading and lock themselves away in a cage of doubt.

Someone who was reliable with a strong desire to help others could become overwhelmed, yet afraid to ask for help themselves.

The best listeners often had no one to talk to. The best talkers often never heard what others told them. For every light, there was a shadow. For every strength, there was a weakness.

Each person I met was unique from anyone else… yet at the same time, no matter our differences, we were all human, and there was no human who could be considered irredeemable or worthless.

Because we were different, there would always be times we would conflict or hurt each other. But because we were all human, we needed to have respect for each person's life and reasoning, even if it might be wrong or confusing.

It was a complicated paradox that I felt I still did not completely understand. But the more I began to grasp at it, the more I wanted to.

"You've been spending a lot of time with Finn, haven't you Mei?" Miyori said with an inquisitive glance one day after class.

The student council president had asked her to introduce Finn to him several weeks prior, but somehow Finn had always managed to dodge her requests.

"Mmm, I guess." I answered, trying not to be pulled into their problems.

"He's been helping me figure out some stuff."

Miyori gave a noncommittal hum, turning back towards the front. "He really seems to be the kind of guy who has to involve himself in everyone's problems doesn't he?"

I tried to get a better look at her while she was distracted.

Miyori's fourth dimension form had always been hard for me to see. Every now and then I would get what looked like fiery red feathers falling around her. When she was upset, I sometimes thought I could see tiny flames igniting along her body — but compared to others I had met, she seemed like a surprisingly blank slate.

When I asked Finn about it, he replied that some people would take more experience to understand. That sometimes you'd need to realize what it was you were seeing before you could see it clearly. When I asked him how he saw Miyori, he simply laughed and changed the subject.

"I wouldn't want to bias you." He had chuckled. "After all, I'm not always right."

I blinked. Miyori's side profile looked the same as it had for all the years I had known her. "Do you not like Finn?" I asked, deciding that I would get more out of her if I was direct.

Miyori leaned back against the desk she was sitting on and looked up at the ceiling as she pondered how to answer.

"It's not that I don't like him," she started. "It's just I think that people like him who meddle in other peoples' private matters do more damage than good."

"Do you think it's wrong to want to help people?" I asked, pushing further.

"It's like helping a baby bird back into its nest, or a butterfly out of its cocoon." Miyori twisted her mouth. "I understand why people want to help when they see a creature struggle. But doing so will only prevent the creature from being strong enough to face the future."

She stood up, picking her bag off the ground.

"No one likes to struggle, but struggling is what helps us grow. I'm sure the guy means well, but at the end of the day, is he really doing what is best for others? Or is he just filling some hero complex to feed his own ego?"

Before I could ponder her question, Miyori's phone rang.

"Ah, sorry Mei. Student council calls." Miyori said to me as she picked up her cell. "We'll have to finish this another time."

Miyori went outside, holding her cell up to her ear. I found myself alone in the empty classroom.

I guess it's time to head home then. I picked up my bag and headed out into the deserted hallways.

Somehow the school always seemed creepy to me when it was empty. It felt as if something could jump out and grab me at any moment.

As I approached the stares, I felt a strong presence seem to grip mercilessly at my heart.

"Who's there?" I cried out, turning to look behind me.

The hallways were still empty, but the air had grown thick. As I squinted, I could see a dark mist beginning to form.

The mist struck terror in my heart, yet I felt somehow drawn towards it. Against my better judgment, I found myself walking towards the source.

I turned the corner and found myself in a shadowy hallway, perforated with innumerable wires drawn taught. They crisscrossed all around me like some gigantic spider's web. As I marveled at the sight, one wire stood out more than the rest. It was thicker than a cable line and shot down the entire length of the hall.

"Aki!" I cried as I followed the cable at a full run.

Turning the corner, I found Aki crouched down on the floor and crying. She clutched her cell phone in both hands and held it close to her chest.

"Aki!" I cried out again, rushing to her side. "What's wrong? What happened to you?"

Aki turned to look up at me with red and teary eyes. When she saw me beside her, the wires protruding from her pulled tight again threatening to tear her apart.

"It's okay Aki!" I comforted. "Just tell me what happened?"

Looking at the ground Aki quickly dried her eyes, before turning towards me with the largest, fakest smile I had seen yet.

"Ah! Mei! You surprised me." She sniffed. "I just got some bad news from home. It seems my mom was caught in a bit of an accident. She's resting in the hospital now."

"Oh... Aki..." I gasped, my eyes beginning to tear up as well, but Aki shook her head before I could say anything else.

"It's all right," she said. "Father said they don't know when mom's going to wake up again... but he said that the best thing I could do for her is to keep working hard so I can tell her all I've done when she does, so... I've got to be strong."

Aki wiped her eyes one last time as she picked up her bag.

"I'm sorry." She gave a forced laugh. "I didn't want anyone to see me like this so I was hiding in this hallway while I rested a bit. But I'm better now. I've got to go to track meet now. I'm sure they're all waiting for me. I don't want to let them down. I'm going to show my mother a big shiny medal when she wakes up!"

"Aki!" I cried reaching out towards her. "Wait!"

I tried to go after her, but she had already run to the end of the hall.

The new wire seemed to be attached straight to her heart. The sheer size of the wire and how tightly it tugged on her... it must have been an unbearable weight to carry.

"Aki..." I sighed, as I watched her disappear around the corner. She clearly didn't want me to get involved. Should I chase after her? What was the right thing to do in a situation like this?

Was Miyori right about needing to let people face hardships themselves? Or was Finn right that we had been given this ability for a reason, and that the world needed people like us to intercede?

I wasn't certain I knew the answer, but what I did know was that watching Aki run away made my heart feel like it was being crushed.

I guess I still have a lot to learn.

As I headed back to the stairs, I was surprised to see how late it had gotten. The sun was already setting. I was probably one of the last students left in the school.

I might not get any homework done tonight. I sulked as I made my way down the stairs. All I wanted to do was go home and take a nap.

I was about to turn down the second half of the staircase when I heard a voice call out from the bottom. To my surprise, my body froze, unable to move any farther.

"I finally caught up with you." The voice sounded relieved.

It was hard to tell, but it seemed to be the voice of our student council president, Yamada Tetsua.

I had only heard him once in a school assembly, but he had a confident, charismatic manner about him that seemed to draw people towards him. He had apparently unanimously won the title of student council president every year that he had attended the school. He was considered wise and kind by students and teachers alike.

"You wouldn't have been dodging me on purpose, now would you?" he asked.

There was no audible response, so I couldn't tell who he was talking to. After a brief pause he continued:

"I've been watching you for quite a while now you know. I'm sure I don't have to tell you how people like you and I have a bit of a gift when it comes to recognizing other... more interesting students."

Yamada paused for emphasis. "I'd like to offer the opportunity to take you on as my own personal *kouhai*. I'm sure with my help you would find yourself able to accomplish far more than you're currently able to on your own."

I shouldn't be here... I thought to myself as I tried to force my legs to make their way back up the stairs. As I made the first step, the second participant finally spoke up.

"Eh, I'm sorry dude." I heard Finn's distinctive, *anime*-inspired Japanese reply. "I ain't got a clue what you're talking about. Besides. I'm really not one for clubs to begin with. Being alone works fine for me."

It was Finn?? But what was he doing here? Did Miyori finally convince him to come? And what was Yamada talking about? Did he know about Finn's abilities? If that was the case, did he know about mine as well?

"Tsk, tsk, tsk." Yamada reprimanded. "You aren't in Canada anymore you know. How much longer do you intend to keep up this independent lone wolf facade of yours?

I get it. I really do. You think that by not making any connections, you won't be able to hurt anyone by accident. You're willing to take on any amount of pain to avoid doing that again."

The president paused for a moment as his manner seemed to change.

"But what if that stubborn will of yours ends up getting those you care about into trouble?"

The air in the hallway changed. It became so thick and heavy that I could hardly breathe. I covered my mouth as I was hit by a wave of energy sending a chill down my spine. I wanted to scream, but was terrified of being caught. It felt as if every fiber of my being was telling me to run for my life, but all the strength had been drained from my legs.

"There! That look!" Yamada laughed. "It's good to see you are taking me seriously at last!"

The tension in the air seemed to lighten slightly, but my legs were still shaking too much to move. For a long while there was nothing but silence.

"Well, you don't have to give me an answer today," Yamada said casually.

"I'll give you some time to consider my offer. But you're a smart kid, despite how you act. I'm sure you'll make the right choice — for everyone's sake."

As the sound of footsteps echoed off into the distance I fell to the ground. My legs had no strength left to stand.

What was this feeling? Was it because of my new abilities? And what was that conversation about? What was the student council president trying to goad Finn into doing? I had so many questions, and no answers for any of them.

I put my hand against my forehead as the weakness seemed to spread throughout my entire body.

"Huh? Mei?" I heard a voice call out from below me.

I looked up and saw Finn standing a few steps beneath me with a confused and worried look on his face.

"What are you doing on the ground?" he asked, running to my side.

CHAPTER SIX
The First Job

"Seriously," Finn sighed, handing me a can of juice from the vending machine. "Why is it I keep finding you lying on the ground? Is that 'anemic' thing from *anime* really that serious?"

"You know that's not really..."

I started to counter him, but it fell short in my throat. I wasn't in the mood for jokes. It had been a long day and I wasn't certain what was what anymore.

Finn watched as I stared blankly at the can in my hands. Turning away, he leaned back against the wall before letting out a sigh.

"I guess you heard all that then?" he said at last.

Assuming he was referring to the argument that just took place, I nodded.

"Ah, I'm really sorry about that." He scratched his head, looking oddly embarrassed. "I got a bit frustrated is all."

I wasn't certain why he was apologizing. He didn't raise his voice or break anything like in American movies. Did it have anything to do with that strange wave of energy I had felt?

"Did he ask something unreasonable?" I asked.

I had never met the student council president, so I had no idea what sort of a guy he was.

Miyori would say he was a reliable man who gave his best for the school, but that description was a bit too vague to give any idea as to his character.

Finn gave an awkward laugh as he tried to force a smile.

"Ah, it was nothing he said. It's just that he's the type of person I tend to clash with."

Finn was acting odd... well odder than usual. It was strange to see him acting so affected.

For as long as he had been at our school, he had taken every type of rudeness and violence tossed at him in his stride. He had always remained his usual, calm, disinterested self no matter how much he hurt inside.

"Ohh?" I peered at him inquisitively. "So even you have people who can get under your skin?"

"Unfortunately so." He replied. He wasn't taking my bait.

Finn let out a deep sigh and took a sip from his own drink. His eyes were directed at the tiles on the floor, but they seemed to be looking at something a million miles away.

"I don't think there is anyone in this world who can get along with everyone," he added, almost to himself. "But, the thing I hate most, is how the hardest people to get along with are usually the ones most like us."

"So you and the student council president are similar?"

"No," he replied flatly. "At least I hope not... not anymore... But who I am, and who I am by nature, aren't always the same thing."

I was starting to feel like this was a topic I had no right to pry into, so I tried to go back on topic.

"What did he ask then?"

Finn took another sip before replying. "He wanted me to check on a shut-in. A guy named Suzuki Raku."

"Suzuki Raku?" I cried out.

Finn returned my shocked outburst with a curious glance.

"Do you know him?" he asked.

I shook my head.

"Not personally, no. But I have heard of him. He's a second year. He used to be an honor student as well as the ace of our basketball team."

"Oh?" Finn said. "Sounds like quite the busy guy."

I shrugged.

"I wouldn't know. Apparently, his grades started slipping towards the end of last year. Soon after, our team started losing their games. I heard around that time he started skipping out on classes and practices, then eventually stopped showing up all together."

"You know a surprising amount about this guy, don't ya?" Finn marveled while shifting nervously away from me.

"It's not like that!" I cried out, punching Finn's arm. "Sheesh. I do talk to people other than you, ya know!"

Finn rubbed his sore arm as I leaned forward hugging my knees.

"He was the talk of the school at the start of the year." I explained. "There were rumors that everything he had accomplished was due to cheating, and that was why he had to run away."

"It never ceases to amaze me how supportive people can be to a fellow student in crisis," Finn sighed in a cynical tone.

Taking a last gulp from his drink, he crushed the can, tossing it in a nearby receptacle.

"So, what are you going to do?" I asked as I got up to join him.

Finn opened his shoe locker to collect his things.

"I dunno." He mused while switching into his outdoor shoes. "Personally, I don't want to give that prez the satisfaction of thinking that he has anything over me… but I guess at the same time, I don't think there's any harm in checking."

I smiled and ran up beside him.

"Let's go then!" I said as we walked out the front doors of the school.

Finn looked at me for moment before giving a slight smirk.

"You've changed you know." He smiled.

"Have I?" I asked. "Miyori and Aki have pointed that out too." I made a thoughtful face, "I still feel like me."

There was a glint of light as Finn tossed a small, round object towards me. Flustered, I somehow managed to catch it without dropping it.

Taking a closer look, I realized it was a small compact mirror.

"Wait…" I questioned. "Why do *you* have something like this?"

"Don't ask questions!" Finn scolded quickly. "Just look at it! You should find it interesting."

Opening the mirror, I saw my own familiar face staring back at me. No strange appendages, weapons, eyeballs, or armor.

"It's just me." I frowned, a little disappointed.

"Try focusing," Finn said. "No one harder to see accurately than yourself."

Squinting slightly, I saw something starting to form above my head. The harder I focused, the clearer it became.

My eyes changed first. They were a bright, vibrant green, instead of their usual brown, and had long, vertical pupils. As my eyes wandered upwards, I noticed something moving on the top of my head.

They were ears. Like Finn's... but not quite like Finn's. They were black and pointy. More like...

"A cat?!" I cried out. Suddenly the eyes made sense.

Finn burst out laughing.

"Seriously? That's what it was??" he laughed. "I always thought you'd end up a bit feline, but I didn't want to sound like I was stereotyping from all the *anime* I watched."

"What kind of *anime* have you been watching!?" I shouted out, hiding my blushing face.

Wait.

Awkwardly I scrambled to angle the tiny compact mirror to see behind me. Sure enough, a long, thin black cat's tail twitched left and right behind me.

Finn was beside himself laughing. I watched as his own tail wagged like mad.

"It's not funny!" I sulked, trying to cover up my embarrassment. "I was hoping I could gain some really cool angel wings or like, a nine-tailed fox look. Now I just feel like I belong in a maid café in Akihabara!

"No, no!" Finn waved his hands in my direction as he tried to force himself to stop laughing. "It suits you! It really does! Attentive, aloof, agile, loyal, yet does what she wants. I think it fits you to a T!"

I looked up at Finn, who stared at me earnestly. He managed to keep a straight face for five whole seconds before he returned to his uncontrollable laughter.

***

Finn rubbed his sore face as he rang the doorbell to Suzuki's house.

"What?" I shot him a glare as he threw another sidelong glance my way.

"Nothing," he replied. "Even I'll admit I had that one coming."

The sound of movement behind the door brought us back to attention as it opened to reveal Suzuki's mother.

She was a little wary of a foreigner like Finn at first, but when I explained that the student council had sent us to talk to her son, she gratefully welcomed us in.

She led us down the hall past old basketball trophies and newspaper clippings to a door that read "Raku" on it. Though the door was identical to all other doors in the apartment, it seemed dim, like a haze had settled over it.

Mrs. Suzuki knocked once, but there was no answer. Giving a slight sigh, she turned towards us with a nod, then flung the door open.

As soon as the door opened, the smell of stale air filled my lungs. The lights were off, the blinds were closed, and the whole room was littered with filthy clothes and empty food wrappers.

The only light in the room came from a lone computer screen on a desk.

As we entered, the tall chair in front of the computer screen turned towards us to reveal a pale boy hunched over in a hoodie.

The mother nodded to us one last time and left silently. We were alone with a very frail-looking Suzuki Raku.

Suzuki squinted at us through sleep deprived eyes, before letting out a sigh and turning back to his computer.

"So, what is it this time?" he asked. "I'll fail my year if I don't go back? I'll be expelled? Someone else has brought forth proof that I cheated on tests or in my games? Whatever. Just leave your papers on the pile and go."

I couldn't read this guy. Had this been happening frequently for him? Or had he just been expecting this day to come?

"Not much fight left in you, is there?" Finn asked as he looked around the room. "Aren't athletes supposed to be known for their tenacity?"

Suzuki shrugged.

"It doesn't matter anymore," he mumbled. "At one point I was on top of the world, but then I slipped and fell off. There's no getting back up there again."

Squinting my eyes, I tried to focus on Suzuki's fourth-dimension form. massive bundle had been sewed into his back. The sheer weight of carrying it seemed to be the cause of his exhaustion and hunched over form.

"Hey, what's that on his back?" I whispered in Finn's ear. "It doesn't seem like it's part of him, but it also doesn't seem to be something he *wants* to have either."

Finn shook his head.

"He's depressed," he answered in a quiet voice. "As life's problems pile onto you one after another, you end up feeling overwhelmed, and totally insufficient to handle everything that lies before you.

You start feeling exhausted all the time. You don't want to see anyone, or anyone to see you. You hate how your life is now, but it feels like taking the risk to move forward would end up crushing you completely. So instead you just sit, as the weight grows heavier, and it becomes even harder to move."

Finn paused for a moment as he kicked a few soda cans aside.

"If Aki's anxiety is like winding a spring until it snaps, then Suzuki's depression is like the spring winding down, when the gears have long been broken."

I watched Suzuki stare blankly at the screen as he bounced rapidly between various forum boards and social media sites waiting for any to update.

My heart felt painfully gripped, much like when I watched Aki run away. He didn't look sad, angry, or upset. He just seemed incredibly... empty.

"How do we help then?" I whispered. In my head, I was still trying to figure out what to do about Aki. Now faced with Suzuki as well, I was beginning to feel completely helpless.

"Mmm, it's a difficult question..." Finn thought as he looked around the room.

"No matter what you can observe, you can't save someone until they want to save themselves.

Even then, by normal methods, he would be given some method to combat his weariness so he could have the energy to try and force the wheels of his life to turn again. Then once he got back into the rhythm of things, they would slowly try to ween him into relying solely on his own strength, and hope that he didn't trip or backslide along the way."

Finn walked up behind Suzuki's chair and raised a clawed hand above the heavy bundle on his back.

"But in our case," Finn smirked, "We have an option that is a bit more unique."

Finn whacked the back of Suzuki's chair, causing him to jump in shock. Turning around, he looked up at Finn with an irritated glare.

"What is it?" Suzuki blurted out with more emotion than I had heard from him since our arrival.

Finn smiled as he leaned in close.

"You don't really want to be like this do you?" he asked, scratching a single claw along the top of the bundle.

Suzuki turned back to his computer screen.

"It doesn't matter. There's no coming back from this. There's no way out of this hole anymore. There's no point in trying to move forward. It's too late for me now. Go away."

Finn grabbed hold of the bundle on Suzuki's back, and pulled it backwards. As he did Suzuki jumped, instantly straightening his posture with wide eyes.

"I didn't ask what was possible," Finn shot back, sterner than before. "I asked what you *want* to be like."

As Finn stared into Suzuki's eyes, they flickered, as if the light inside them was trying to reignite.

Neither was saying anything, but it was as though Finn was trying to relight the flame in Suzuki's soul through willpower alone.

Suzuki stuttered as his mind fought against his heart.

"I... It's... But... There's..." Tears started to form in the corners of his eyes as he lay his head down against his desk attempting to run away again.

"What do you want?" Finn demanded, pulling Suzuki back by gripping the bundle tighter. "Forget logic. Forget what's possible. Tell me what you *want* to be!"

"I... I don't want to be like this..." Suzuki cried out in a quiet and strained voice. "I don't want any of this... but there's just too much for me to take on anymore."

No sooner had Suzuki confessed, then the bundle on his back began to peel open.

Wasting no time, Finn shot his clawed hand deep into the bundle and began to search.

"No wonder you think that." Finn exclaimed to Suzuki as he forced his way deeper into the bundle, "Just look at how much of a burden you've tried carrying on your shoulders!"

Finn began pulling various objects out of the bundle and throwing them one by one onto the ground.

"You have to be the best player on your team or you're worthless. You have to be the best student in your class or you're a failure. You have to make sure no one questions where you've been all this time. You have to push yourself harder than anyone else. What do you think you are? A super Saiyan??"

"WELL WHAT WOULD YOU HAVE ME DO!?" Suzuki screamed unexpectedly as he leapt to his feet, knocking Finn back. "PEOPLE RELIED ON ME! AND I LET THEM DOWN! I let them all down."

Suzuki fell back into his chair burying his face into his arms and crying.

Finn sat on the floor silently for a few minutes before looking up again.

"So what?" He retorted.

Suzuki looked a little shocked at Finn's cold response.

"If you can't be perfect, people will fail?" Finn asked. "If people fail, it's entirely your fault? This world was never resting on your shoulders to begin with! Why do—"

"WHAT DO YOU KNOW?" Suzuki screamed even louder leaping up from his chair once again. "I'VE NEVER MET YOU BEFORE TODAY! AND WHAT ARE YOU? A FIRST YEAR?? A *GAIJIN*!?!? DON'T THEY TEACH YOU TO RESPECT YOUR ELDERS WHERE YOU'RE FROM!? WHAT WOULD YOU KNOW!? WHAT WOULD YOU UNDERSTAND!? WHAT RIGHT DO YOU HAVE TO COME IN HERE AND BRING THESE THINGS UP TO ME!?"

Finn stood there in silence as Suzuki continued to yell at him. He flinched as each word thrown out seemed to hit him like a stone. But still he stood and listened.

Suzuki gasped for air between tears and he fell against Finn's chest. He seemed exhausted, and unable to think of anything else to say.

Finn smiled as he placed a hand on Suzuki's shoulder. The bundle I could still see on Suzuki's back had deflated slightly during the argument. Had Finn been trying to provoke Suzuki to see if he still had any fighting spirit?

"I don't know," Finn said at last.

Suzuki looked up at him, uncertain how to respond anymore.

Finn took a deep breath and he closed his eyes. "I don't know you."

He continued, "I don't know who you are. I don't know what you grew up with, what people have said to you, what you went through last year. I don't know what you're thinking right now, what you're hoping for your future, or anything about what brought you to this point."

Finn opened his eyes again. His usual, lackluster expression was gone. His eyes were burning like an intense and passionate flame. They seemed to cut through the dark mist which had enveloped the room like the morning sun.

"But here's what I do know." His voice, full of conviction, echoed around the silent room, "I know what it's like to believe you've let people down. I know what it's like to believe you have no future left. To wake up every morning and want your life to feel different, but believing there's no way you can ever go back again. To not want to wake up at all. To wonder if you even deserve to be happy again.

I know what it feels like… and I know I never want to let anyone face that feeling alone again."

The room was silent as Suzuki and I stared at Finn in disbelief. Finn was breathing heavily as sweat ran down his brow, but the intensity in his eyes remained constant.

"What do I do?" Suzuki asked after a long pause. "How do I go back to how things were?"

Finn let out a deep breath as his emotions seemed to calm.

"You can't." He turned towards the window.

"Time can't move back. It only goes forward. You can never go back to how things were, but as long as you are alive, you can decide how you want to move forward."

"And how is one supposed to go forward?" Suzuki asked beginning to get annoyed again.

Finn placed a hand on Suzuki's shoulder, letting his claw push into the stitches on the bundle.

"One step at a time." He gave a sympathetic smile.

"Don't worry about getting the best grades. Just try to get to school and learn what you can. Don't worry about winning every game. Worry about showing up to practices and improving the areas where you are weak. Don't lose sleep over what people will say about who you were. Strive to become someone who outshines your past self in every way.

You can't change the past, but you can work for a better future. You can't guarantee you'll ace every test, but if you even get five questions right out of one hundred, that's five things you wouldn't have known if you hadn't spent that time studying."

As I watched Finn talk, I could see the stitches of the bundle slowly burn away.

"You can't win every game, but where would be the fun if you could? Let the bitter taste of defeat drive you to try even harder for next time! Your value doesn't come from what you do, or what others say about you.

You are alive. Therefore, you're already invaluable and irreplaceable. Stop worrying about living up to other people's expectations! Grow into the unique you that goes far beyond their expectations!"

When Finn had finished, the last of the stitches burnt away and the bundle fell to the ground where it seemed to melt into the floor.

With the intervention over, we excused ourselves from the house. Suzuki's mother stared at us suspiciously as we said our farewells. It was to be expected, given the amount of shouting we had caused she was liable to be suspicious.

No doubt she would have to apologize to her neighbors after this, but she would most likely consider it worth it once she saw her son.

Finn was oddly quiet as we walked away from the house.

"What will happen to him now?" I asked as we headed down the residential streets.

Finn didn't answer right away. It seemed like he was unsure if he wanted to answer or not.

"It's hard to say," he said after much deliberation. "All I did was give him a chance. Encouragement and hope. They're the only abilities I've ever been able to use really.

I made him realize his burden wasn't as heavy as he felt it was, and I showed him that he was stronger than he thought... but that doesn't necessarily mean he'll take the chance. The rest at this point is up to him."

Finn rubbed his eyes with a yawn. They looked bloodshot and tired.

"You can influence people, but you can't control them." He added, "In a way I'm pretty thankful for that... but at times like this I wish I could do more.

Will he act? Will he start to pick the stresses he let go of back up again? Will he get discouraged at the first person who knocks him down? There's so much that is out of our hands."

I smiled as I watched him stretch.

"Still," I said walking a little ahead of him. "He knows now that someone believes in him, and that's got to count for something."

A small smile came across Finn's face as I turned around to face him.

"You may be right." He replied.

CHAPTER SEVEN

The Pervert

A few weeks later, Suzuki returned to classes.

At first the whole school was abuzz with stories of his return, very few of which were positive. Students took bets on how long it would take before he would run away again. Many still believed that he had been a cheater all along.

But Suzuki proved stronger than the students' lack of faith in him. Though he was no longer an honor student or ace of the basketball team, he took each day at a time and each day that passed seemed to be easier on him than the one before.

He was neither a bad enough student to be ridiculed, nor a good enough student to be praised. Over time, people grew bored of their gossip and allowed him to become just 'another student' in their eyes.

Still, he seemed much happier than before.

He would often stop Finn or myself to say hello. Though he was not the most outgoing or energetic in his class, there was a small fire burning in his eyes which seemed to grow every time we met.

Aki, on the other hand, was a different matter.

The wires attached to her seemed to grow thicker and more numerous every day.

She could barely keep her eyes open. They seemed to plead for an escape. The mask she wore to hide her true emotions was beginning to decay away making it appear even more unnerving than before. Even the once perky rabbit ears of her fourth-dimension form were now wilted, battered and bent.

I had tried numerous times to talk things out with her. To get her to open up to me. But every time I tried, the wires would pull her violently away.

If only I could get her to stay in one spot long enough to say what I wanted to say, but was I right to force myself upon her when she didn't want my help?

Even Miyori was beginning to show signs of concern. She had tried several times to talk to Aki, but each time it was as if words failed her.

Miyori's fourth dimension self was beginning to show. As much as she tried to hide it, I would occasionally see smoke rising from her as her body began to glow like burning embers. I wanted to talk to her as well, but what could I say? If I revealed anything about what I could see, she would think I had gone crazy, and she had enough on her mind right now.

The tension between the three of us seemed to grow every day. We hardly talked anymore which was the most painful part of all.

Miyori would say that it was because of student council, while Aki would claim she had to prepare for her track meet… but we all knew the reality. We were drifting apart.

It wasn't because we cared less for each other. If anything, it was because we cared for each other too much that the awkwardness felt so painful. As much as I hated the current situation, I had no clue what I could do to stop it.

I'd had friends drift away before, and it had always been painful, but this time around, every awkward glance they gave was like carving a knife into my heart.

Was it because of my new awareness? Or was it because these two meant so much to me? We had been friends for as long as I could remember. We had experienced so much together. I couldn't imagine life with us apart. I didn't want to!

I found myself once again waiting for class to start as Aki sat silently beside me, neither of us talking, each afraid to speak up.

"All right ya brats! In yer' seats! Time to get this day movin'!" Ms. Koba rang off, breaking me from my thoughts.

Placing her books on the table, she took a deep breath before turning towards the class.

"I know it's hard to believe, but looks like we've got another transfer student," she explained.

A murmur of excitement rose in the class as everyone considered the exciting possibilities this new transfer student could hold. The excitement died quickly however, as all eyes eventually turned back towards Finn. We were not about to have our hopes destroyed like that twice in one year.

"Just to let you know, he ain't a *gaijin* this time around," Ms. Koba continued, "He's Japan born and bred, but I hope y'all will treat him with the same level of respect I asked for last time."

The teacher shot a quick glare to Tanaka who averted his eyes begrudgingly before she walked to the door to fetch our new classmate. The air was tense as everyone braced themselves for the reveal.

"All right, get in here!" Ms. Koba called as she opened the door.

Eyes widened as our new classmate walked in.

He was a tall boy, well-built, with chiseled features. He walked in a confident stride, with a smile that would melt the hardest of hearts. He wore the same uniform as the rest of us, yet somehow, he made it look like high fashion.

"Hello everyone!" he said with a bow. "My name is Matsuda Yuta. I have recently moved here from Chiba. I am still new to this area and don't know many people yet, but I will do my best to be a classmate worthy of you all. I hope we will all get to be the best of friends. Thank you!"

The class applauded nearly to the point of a standing ovation. His entire introduction was as opposite from Finn's as it could possibly have been. It seemed at last we had finally got the cute transfer student of my dreams.

I think I'm in lo-

My thoughts were cut short as a familiar chill went down my spine. It was a tension and terror I hadn't felt since that day in the stairwell.

Putting my hand to my mouth to hold back a scream, I quickly turned towards Finn.

A deadly fire raged in Finn's eyes as he stared at Matsuda. His fists were clenched, he was grinding his teeth, and the ears on top of his head were pulled back. He looked like a wolf ready to attack, but why?

Turning back to Matsuda, I focused my eyes in order to give him a closer look.

At first, I saw nothing out of the ordinary. Something about his smile seemed a little off, but looking at him made my heart flutter, making it difficult to focus.

I took a deep breath to calm myself and then tried again, putting my feelings aside. As his fourth-dimension form became clear to me, I began to see what Finn was so upset about.

His face was covered by a mask, much like Aki's, only thicker. It had no features save for a large painted on smile and two painted on eyes. Below his face I saw what appeared to be long cords hanging off from his body, much like Tohka's vines, but these cords seemed to be much thicker, and without thorns. At first, I thought I had simply met the male version of Tohka. Upon closer inspection however, I learned the horrifying truth.

My gaze followed the cords to the girls around me, who all seemed to be lost in dreams and fantasies of their own. It seemed as though I might have been right after all, but something still seemed off.

The girls were squirming, and seemed uncomfortable. Something was affecting them that even they didn't realize.

Turning back to the cords, I forced myself to focus on them. They were not vines at all, but long, flesh-coloured tentacles which were slithering their way to all the girls throughout the classroom.

The thorns on Tohka's vines were meant to lock onto the hearts of men, never letting go as she collected them like pets. They were designed to entrap and hold. Matsuda's tentacles however, were just the opposite.

These tentacles were slippery and smooth. Large, bloodshot eyeballs sat at the end of each of them.

While they wormed their way around the bodies of every girl in the classroom, it was not to trap them and hold onto their hearts, but instead to position themselves to get the best lewd angles of their bodies.

I covered my mouth again. This time because I felt like vomiting. The thought that he could so demoralize these girls without even physically touching them was sickening.

I felt my heart stand still I felt something cold and clammy brush up against my own leg. Looking down, I was horrified to see a tentacle eyeball worming its way up between my legs towards the hem of my skirt.

By some miracle I managed to refrain from shrieking. As Matsuda's eyes slowly scanned the entirety of the class, he no longer appeared confident and charismatic, but smug and lustful. He was like a spoiled child looking over a box of chocolates and wondering which ones he should devour first.

Channeling all my frustrations into my leg I stomped on the tentacle and then kicked it out of the way. I felt an immense amount of satisfaction as I heard a slight shriek as the tentacle slithered away. But that satisfaction did not last long as I realized my mistake.

No sooner had I kicked the tentacle away, then Matsuda's eyes locked straight onto me. He stared intently at me as if to determine if I had truly figured him out or if it was just by chance. I expected to see him panic, but instead his face spread into a smile like a predator that had finally found a prey that amused him.

The teacher thanked Matsuda for his introduction, and sent him to his seat.

He was given a desk at the back of class, much to his delight. With him behind me, I felt as if his stares were digging their way through my back.

I felt exposed and helpless as I watched the tentacles continue to spread throughout the classroom.

None of the girls could focus during class. They shifted awkwardly, adjusting their skirts and clothing as tentacles slithered their way over every inch of their bodies.

Though they could not see the tentacles, and most likely did not realize it was Matsuda who was making them feel this way, they seemed to instinctively realize they were in danger.

I had told myself I would just try to ignore the tentacles the next time they came to me. I had already grabbed his attention once, and I didn't want to encourage his interest in me. But I just couldn't do it!

Every time I saw the disgusting eyeballs slither their way towards me I would panic and shift, or try to knock them away. Each time I did, I felt Matsuda's interest in me grow stronger. It was as if I could feel him breathing down my back.

At one point I hazarded a glance back at him, just to make sure I wasn't imagining things.

He was staring straight at me, but not with a look of frustration or panic. He seemed completely amused watching his prey's futile attempts to escape. Of all the things wrong with Matsuda, his unshakeable confidence was by far, the most terrifying.

Finn never spoke up, but sat with his chin resting in his arms. His eyes were not dead and lackluster like they usually were. It seemed as if it was taking all his strength to hold back the inferno which burned within them.

***

"Why didn't you say anything?" I asked Finn at lunch. I was feeling exhausted, frustrated, and uncomfortable.

"I know you've noticed it, so don't try to deny it. You look like you're ready to kill. You don't have to do anything lethal, but I'm not about to stop you."

Finn was still staring at Matsuda. As if he were waiting for the right moment to pounce. Letting out a sigh of defeat, he turned back to me.

"You're forgetting the annoying point that not everyone can see the fourth dimension." He sounded even more frustrated than I was.

"What has he *done* so far? He hasn't attacked anyone. He hasn't touched anyone. He hasn't said anything rude or out of line. He hasn't even physically stared at anyone in a way that we could use against him!

Remember the reaction the class had when I fought with Tanaka? If our classmates were that supportive of a hot head like him, how much more so do you think they will be for a charismatic monster like that?"

Finn pointed to where Matsuda sat with a bright, warm smile, surrounded by the majority of the class.

"I see! You were the class rep back at your old school?" Oga inquired in his usual sincere manner. "That would explain why your dress and mannerisms are so exact and proper! If you don't mind, I would love to hear your advice in my endeavors to improve our class!"

"Matsuda! Matsuda!" another boy called out. "I heard you had three sports teams fighting over you in your old school! And that you made it to nationals in Judo! Are you considering joining any of our teams? I know the basketball team could definitely use a guy like you!"

"Matsuda?" one of the girls shyly interjected. "If you want someone to show you around campus, I'd be more than happy to."

Finn let out another sigh as the bombardment of questions and comments continued.

"People like that are as dangerous as they come." He groaned. "They're attractive, athletic, and academic. Raise an argument against them and they'll have you believing you were the one in the wrong before you know it. A person like that could steal your wallet and you would end up thanking them for it."

"But how?" I asked. "The guys being dense I can accept... but I was watching during class. The girls were squirming as he kept leering at them. How have they not caught on yet? Why are they still trying to win him over?"

Finn shrugged.

"It's Charisma. In all honesty, I've never understood how it works. But it's a talent I'm both envious and terrified of."

"Charisma?" I asked. "But I don't see anything on him save for those perv-tentacles."

Finn shook his head.

"I've never been able to pinpoint it either. No matter what angle you look at it from, there's no real difference between a normal and a charismatic person.

They don't have to be attractive, or talented, or have a good voice, or be confident... yet somehow the rules of society never seem to apply to them.

Whether it be by making demands, getting away with wrongdoings, having insults laughed off... a charismatic person can not only be put up with, but agreed with no matter what they do."

Finn let out another deep sigh as he fell against his desk.

"In most cases charismatic people never realize the advantages they have going for them," he continued. "In fact, charismatic people are usually the least empathetic people you'll meet. They just can't clue in to how the world is *supposed* to work as they've rarely experienced it themselves.

But when a charismatic person comes to understand what power they wield… and instead of treating it with respect, they decide to wield it to its full potential… that is a terrifying person to face."

"So what? Do we do nothing?" I cried out in frustration.

Finn thought for a moment before answering.

"I can't win an argument with him." He shook his head. "If I was to confront him head on, it would take him five minutes to prove that all my problems with him are due to my own immaturity. In a worst-case scenario, he could play the victim card and turn the entire class against us. In that case we would lose all chances to help anyone until it was too late."

I stared at him helplessly, but he added, "There is one other lead I want to check with first. I doubt it will accomplish anything, but I want to try it."

Finn caught me off guard as he grabbed me by the wrist.

"But believe me," he stared straight into my eyes an intensity that made my face go pale. "The moment he relaxes and decides he can make his move, I will come down on him with a fury so fierce, it will make him regret ever stepping foot into this classroom!"

He said this to comfort me, but the dark flames which seemed to resonate from him were beginning to scare me.

***

Matsuda was still surrounded by students by the end of the day.

Finn seemed to be able to take it no longer as he marched out of the classroom in a huff. Only I seemed to notice, though.

Miyori and Aki both left for their respective afterschool activities without so much as a nod in my direction. I let out a sigh as I watched them leave. Was our friendship really this far beyond repair?

With no one else to talk to, and no real desire to be near Matsuda anymore, I quietly gathered my books and left the classroom alone.

The world seemed so empty as I made my way home. It was either because I left school so early, or because my mind was too distracted to notice anything around me.

I wasn't thinking about where I was going. I didn't really care how long it took me to get home. My mind was full, and I wanted to work through it. So much was going on right now. I had no clue what I was supposed to focus on first.

I found myself stopping in front of a dark alleyway.

This was where it all began.

I had not been here since the incident with Tanaka. Somehow, the shortcut didn't seem worth it anymore. But this was the place where my whole adventure had started.

This was where I first saw the fourth dimension. The place where I first interacted with Finn. The place where I first realized how dangerous our internal struggles could be.

If I had never come here… If I had never gained this ability… would things have been different? Would my friendships with Aki and Miyori be stronger?

I turned to head back, but before I could leave, a strong hand clasped firmly over my mouth.

The world around me seemed to spin as I was dragged against my will deep into the alleyway. I couldn't breathe or move. Each time I came close to regaining my balance my assailant would readjust his grip on me throwing me off kilter yet again.

I let out a gasp for air as I was thrown face first against the rough cement. My clothes tore and my elbow was bleeding, but I had no time to think about these things.

No sooner had I hit the ground then I felt the weight of a heavy body on top of me. I was panicked and in pain as I was forcibly flipped over to find myself face to face with my attacker. It was Matsuda!

"You little tease," he sneered as he stroked his fingernail along my cheek. "You've been avoiding my gaze all day! You like leading a man on, don't you?"

Every time I tried to scream I found his hand clamped firmly over my mouth again. The tentacle eyes were wrapping themselves around every part of me, digging their way under my clothes. I wanted to scream, I wanted to cry, but he wouldn't let me.

In desperation I bit hard into his hand, causing him to pull back. I took the opportunity to send a swift kick into his side. I thought I had managed to escape as he began to lose his balance, but to my horror, the way he landed only made it harder to move.

"Oh ho ho!" he reveled as he mockingly shook his bleeding hand. "You like to do it rough I see. I'm not against a girl with a bit of fight to her."

He leaned in so close that I could feel his breath.

"But I should warn you. I made it to the nationals in Judo last year, and I'm familiar with three other forms of martial art as well. I doubt even that muscle-head Tanaka in our class could hold his own against me."

"Y-You'll never get away with this!" I cried as he began to run his fingers along my body. "P-people will find out! I-I'll tell them tomorrow! I-I'll never let you do this to anyone else again!"

"Y-y-you'll I-I-I'll," he mocked with a laugh. "You're trembling far too much to be a threat my dear."

I let out a cry of pain as he changed his grip on my body. My bones felt like they would break if I tried to move at all.

"Go ahead and tell them," he whispered as licked along my cheek. "Didn't you see them today? They all love me. They all think I'm an angel. And you? I didn't see anyone come up to talk to you today. You're just a nobody. That's why I chose you."

His face twisted in a malicious grin, "Say whatever you want. I'll just say you made it all up. I'll say you confessed your love to me and I turned you down, and now you're trying to get back at me."

He let out another laugh.

"People are so easy. You'd be surprised how often that works. All it takes is a shy smile and a dig at your credibility and they'll all fall back to me every time."

"No…" I sobbed, tears running down my cheeks as I fought in vain. "I don't want this."

My arms and legs gained scrapes and bruises as I struggled to find a way to get myself free. The joints popped and I felt like my limbs were going to be ripped off. But even still, his grip would not give way.

"Now then," he licked his lips and leaned forward, "time for my meal."

CHAPTER EIGHT
The Collar Breaks

No sooner had the final bell rung, when Finn grabbed his already packed bag and marched off into the hall.

The halls were empty as most students were taking their time, chatting with friends, or organizing their things before heading to a club. Finn however continued his hasty march past them all.

He navigated the various halls and stairwells until he found himself standing in front of the student council office.

Yamada Tetsua looked up from his papers as Finn threw open the door. The rest of the student council were still in their respective classrooms, so the room was empty, but the disturbance was still something he could have done without.

"Oh. Finn Coller wasn't it? What brings you here today?" Yamada asked in his usual polite manner.

"What do you want with me Yamada?" Finn shot out, slamming the door behind him.

The student council president took off his glasses and gave Finn a perplexed look.

"What do I want?" he sounded confused. "You were the one who walked in here. Would that not suggest that it is *you* who wants something from me?"

A loud bang echoed through the room as Finn slammed his hands down onto Yamada's desk.

"DON'T MESS WITH ME!" Finn shouted. "What do you want? Why are you targeting me?! What about me is making you feel so threatened??"

Yamada smiled as he rested his chin on his folded hands.

"Careful." He warned, "Your true face is starting to show again."

Finn's eyes widened as Yamada casually grabbed the fourth-dimension collar around his neck between two fingers and began to tug.

In one swift movement, Finn slapped Yamada's hand away and took a leap backwards into some desks, holding his hand against his throat.

"Oh?" Yamada smirked. I just wanted to adjust it for you. Doesn't that feel a little too tight?"

Finn began to tremble as Yamada rose from his seat, casually making his way towards him.

"I know what you are," Yamada explained. "I know your past. I know what you became. I know what you're trying to hide from everyone around you."

Desks were shoved haphazardly out of the way as Finn retreated further back, but Yamada's pursuit remained steady and unchanging.

"Who do you think you are fooling with this lone wolf act?" he asked. "You threw all that away. You became something greater. You became something far more powerful. Something far more interesting.

Why keep up this farce? Do you think you can protect people by hiding what you really are? Do you think by pushing them away they won't get close enough to see what you're hiding? Do you think you're saving them from becoming what you are?"

Finn clawed at his neck as the collar began to pulse, but Yamada continued his assault.

"Do you honestly think you've changed? That you got a second chance? No matter how tight you make that collar, no matter what face you show those around you... The real you is still waiting deep inside. You can go on hiding all you want, but you'll never be anything more than a fake."

He tilted his head, still holding eye contact. "One day you'll slip. You'll let down your guard. You'll convince yourself there might still be a place for you in this world."

Placing his hand on the wall behind Finn, Yamada leaned in close.

"And when the real you starts to surface, everyone whom you had the gall to bring close to you will burn and suffer for your pride."

The sound of tables clattering filled the classroom as Finn plowed through the desks and charged out the door, still clinging to his neck.

"F-Finn!" Miyori cried out as Finn nearly ran her over in the doorway. Finn however, never paused. He ran down the hall as fast as his legs could carry him.

"What was that about?" Miyori asked Yamada, who was leaning casually against the wall.

Yamada shrugged as he returned to his desk. Reaching down below, he pulled out a bag of wasabi candies.

"I challenged the *gaijin* to a contest." He smiled, putting his glasses back on. "I never thought he would push himself so far though. Poor guy is probably running for the washroom."

"I see..." Miyori said as she began straightening the desks in the room.

For a while neither said anything. Miyori cleaned the classroom while Yamada focused on his paperwork.

After some time had passed, Miyori spoke up, "Yamada, sir."

Yamada looked up at her but did not say anything.

"You wouldn't hide anything from us, correct?" she asked after a long pause.

Yamada examined her face as he readjusted his glasses.

"Do you have a reason to think I am hiding anything from you?" he asked in reply.

For a long while, Yamada and Miyori both remained silent as they stared at each other.

"No. Of course not." Miyori broke her gaze and turned back to her own desk. "I apologize, I don't know what came over me."

***

As club events commenced for the evening, the students of the school took part in their usual daily activities, completely unaware of what was happening in a back alley nearby.

Had it been later in the day, there might have been a slight chance of someone happening by such an out of the way location. But since I had decided to leave early, most of the students were still at school, and the surrounding streets were empty.

No… even if they weren't empty, would anyone come looking for me? I couldn't cry out. And who would notice if I disappeared?

Matsuda was right. Aki and Miyori had moved on in their lives without me. They were always so awkward around me these days. They wouldn't come looking for me. They would just be thankful I wasn't around.

I looked up at Matsuda. Drool began to drip from his mouth as the mask shattered and fell to the ground beside me. His teeth were sharp and his eyes were large and bloodshot like the eyes of the numerous tentacles that had me entrapped.

His consciousness was slipping. It was like what I had seen happen to Tanaka when I met him in this same alleyway. He had lost his ability to reason. He was rapidly turning into a monster. A beast driven by carnal desires like lust and pride.

"Now then." Matsuda said licking his lips with a long and narrow tongue while leaning in towards my body. "Time for my meal!"

I clenched my eyes tightly as his lips came towards my body, but his advances were halted as something fell a few feet away.

Opening my eyes, I saw Matsuda sitting upright, straddling my waist between his legs and staring back towards the entrance of the alleyway.

Following his gaze, I saw a familiar set of wolf ears standing upright on a shaggy head of hair.

It was Finn. His shoulders had fallen lax causing his bag to slide onto the ground, and his tail hung limp behind him. His eyes were wide, and his mouth was slightly agape as he looked towards us.

I started to call his name, but something seemed wrong.

Was this really Finn? His eyes were staring in our direction, but his mind seemed distant. He didn't move, and his eyes seemed locked in the same position unblinking.

Matsuda even began to feel uncomfortable as he began to look around like a desperate animal.

The air around us grew thicker and warmer, and steam began to rise from the ground. It became hard to breathe. As if the very air itself tasted like death.

As scared as I felt with Matsuda attacking me, it paled in comparison to the panic that gripped my heart now. It was as if every fiber of my being was screaming for me to get out of there, but every ounce of strength had been drained from my body.

It was at this point that I noticed Finn's collar. It had begun pulsing, as hot steam rose from it.

With each pulse, the collar grew looser, and the air around us grew thicker. The tag on the front no longer read 'Fear'. It cycled through numerous words, changing faster and faster as the pulses came quicker and quicker.

'Anger, Doubt, Confusion, Panic, Guilt, Fear, Fury, Sadness—'. Word after word appeared on the tag, which started to glow white like molten hot metal.

"What?" Matsuda scoffed, regaining some composure as he realized Finn was not moving. "What are you looking at *gaijin*? She was asking for this all day. Don't look at me like I'm some criminal or something!"

The cycling words on Finn's tag finally rested on a dark red Kanji. One that read 'Bloodlust'. With a flash light, the tag itself shattered into tiny fragments which seemed to vanish into the air.

With the tag gone, the collar immediately grew to the size of a large hoop hovering around Finn's neck.

At the same time, two flaming dragon wings burst out of his back in a fiery explosion. The alley was flooded with a raging inferno. The pressure in the air was unbearable!

We are going to die... I found the words entered my mind subconsciously. It wasn't fear or pessimism. It was a fact I had suddenly accepted.

Forcing my eyes back onto Finn, it was nearly impossible to see him through the massive inferno of death and despair that radiated around him. Somehow, I managed to focus enough to catch a glimpse of his glowing eyes, though it took all my willpower to manage it.

I could no longer see Finn in his eyes... It was like staring into the eyes of some creature... no... of a force of nature itself.

"Oh I get it," Matsuda boasted, forcing a smile, though his voice was beginning to crack. "You wanted this one to yourself! Well too bad! No use crying just because you didn't have the-"

Matsuda's words were cut short as the weight on top of me was suddenly lifted.

Picking myself up onto my elbows, I looked down the alleyway to see Matsuda lying on the ground, and Finn standing in front of him, his head cocked to one side.

Wait, I thought as I patted myself down. *Matsuda is no longer on top of me...*

Matsuda's *physical* body was no longer on top of me...

Up until this point I had gotten used to seeing people's fourth dimensional forms moving separate of their physical bodies. Insults, threats, encouragement, emotions. These tactics could have impact on the fourth dimensional body faster than the eye could track.

I had seen it happen so many times that I didn't stop to question it. But this time was different.

Finn *physically* moved faster than my eyes could track. Finn *physically* knocked Matsuda off me and down the alleyway. Finn *physically* kicked a national-level Judo champion down to the ground in a single moment.

As I tried to steady myself, my hand landed on something gross. I looked down and was shocked to see several scorched tentacles that had been forcefully torn from Matsuda's body writhing as they dissolved into the ground.

A physical, AND psychological attack? I gasped and stumbled back as I watched the dying tentacles crumble to ash.

Matsuda groaned, "Ugh, what happened?" and started to roll over. He stopped when he saw Finn standing before him.

"That was pretty good." He smirked and sat upright again. "You actually got a clean hit on me. But—"

Matsuda went to pull Finn's legs out from under him, but once again, he was too slow.

Finn jumped several feet up in the air, landing against the wall on all fours. Another jump sent him in the air directly above Matsuda. With a final kick, he shot himself straight down. His feet landed heavily onto Matsuda's arms with a blood curdling *crack*.

Matsuda let out a scream as his arms bent the wrong way under Finn's weight, but Finn wasn't done yet.

Kneeling heavily on Matsuda's shoulders, Finn began pummeling away at Matsuda, forcefully tearing his fourth dimensional form away from his physical body at an unbelievably high speed.

Dismembered tentacles and blood flew this way and that as Finn, like a wild beast, violently tore apart the fabric of Matsuda's very being.

The scene was like something out of a horror picture. Matsuda's cries made me feel sick to my stomach. But the scariest thing of all was the look in Finn's eyes.

There was no hatred, fear, pity, or compassion within them. They were empty. Unblinking. Like his very humanity had been forcibly torn out.

"THAT'S ENOUGH, FINN!" I shouted. My feet began moving on their own and I tackled him from the side.

As we went down he lowered himself into a roll, and kicked my body into the air. I cried out in pain as I rolled against the rough cement, but I had no time to catch myself before Finn landed on top of me.

With me pinned down below him, he pulled back his fist to punch my face. I cringed as his hand came towards me, but it stopped halfway.

"Finn," I gasped, looking up at him.

Tears had begun streaming down Finn's face. His teeth were clenched and his arm was shaking. The collar, which had up to this point made a perfect ring orbiting his neck, began to warp, as it fought between expanding or contracting.

"Fight it!" I cried out. "This isn't you, Finn! You know it isn't! I believe in you!"

The light fought to return to Finn's eyes as I saw a frustration and sadness within them that I could barely comprehend.

His fist was still shaking, as though he were fighting his own body in order to protect me.

With one last primal scream, Finn changed the angle of his fist, and sent it flying full force into the side of his own face.

I looked on in horror as Finn bounced off the ground several times, before landing unconscious.

The collar instantly shrunk back tightly around his neck. Instead of a tag, the spiked studs which had lined the collar turned around, nailing themselves deep into Finn's throat.

"FINN!" I scrambled to get to his side.

My clothes were torn and filthy, and my arms and legs were bruised and bleeding, but somehow, I had ended up the least injured person in the alleyway.

Matsuda lay on his back breathing heavily. I couldn't tell if he was still conscious, but he seemed unresponsive to anything going on around him. Finn lay sprawled on the ground with his eyes shut. The side of his head bleeding from the blow, his arms and legs bent in unnatural ways.

Putting my ear close to Finn's face, I confirmed he was still breathing. With a sigh I fell back onto my heels, unsure whether to be relieved or devastated.

Almost absentmindedly, I found my hand moving towards Finn's collar.

I had always thought it was strange, but Finn had always dodged any questions I raised about it.

Curiosity getting the better of me, I pushed two fingers between the collar and his neck and tried to tug on it.

Instantly, my mind was filled with a multitude of images and memories.

Was this Finn's life?

I saw a five-year-old Finn walking away from a girl in a wheelchair with his parents.

"We're so proud of you, sweetie!" his mother said cheerfully, leading the young Finn by the hand. "There are so many kids who are too scared to talk to girls like her since she can't speak for herself. I'm sure it meant a lot to her for you to spend time with her like that."

"It did!" young Finn replied with a bright smile as he skipped down the road. "Didn't you see her? She was really really deep in there, but she was so happy to meet someone could see her!"

"Oh, Finn." His father laughed. "You always say the strangest things."

The scene shifted to young Finn crying as his mother and a teacher were looking on with concern.

"It hurts! The teacher hurt me so much!" the boy sobbed.

"I don't understand what's wrong." The teacher desperately tried to explain. "I just scolded him for leaving the Grade 1 playground, when he fell down and started crying like this!"

"Now, Finn," his mother reprimanded. "You've got to stop being so sensitive. The teacher didn't do anything wrong. Stop being such a problem for other people!"

Young Finn continued crying while clutching at his heart even harder.

The scene shifted to a slightly older Finn being scolded by his parents in another situation.

"Why are you fighting us so much on this?" his mother cried out. "We're just going to see our neighbor's new pool. It was very nice of them to invite us over!"

"NO!" Finn screamed. "I don't wanna go there! It all feels wrong when he's there! He feels icky!"

"Finn, we talked about this." His mother's voice took on a warning tone. "You can't get feelings from people. You're just working yourself up over nothing to try and prove that you're some special case. It's not healthy for you! You need to let go of these foolish fantasies!"

The scene switched again and I saw Finn in a school counselor's office.

"Finn," the counselor began, "you have an overactive imagination, paranoia, depression, anxiety, and no attention span.

I will be honest with you, it is unlikely you will ever make it to high school...

This really should have been caught several years ago. But I want you to take this prescription to your parents. With their permission, we might be able to make a way for you hang in until the seventh grade."

As Finn left the room, he crumbled the paper in frustration and threw it into a nearby garbage can. The scenes switched again.

"Don't talk to that kid," a junior high classmate whispered. "He's a weirdo. He goes up to people he doesn't know and acts like he's their best friend!"

"Ugh, I know!" another shot back. "When he was talking to me he asked me about stuff I haven't even told my best friends yet. He must be some sort of stalker or something!"

Again, I saw a junior high Finn. He was walking down the street, when he suddenly stopped near an empty alley. It didn't look much different from where we were currently.

"Where are you!" he cried out. "Where are you!? I feel you hurting!!! Where are you!?"

He ran down the unlit alley until he saw a man being mugged by two thugs.

"I-I called the cops!" he cried out to the two thugs. "T-They'll be here any minute! Y-You'd better run!"

The two thugs laughed as they looked at Finn, who was shaking with his fists raised.

"Little punk!" the first shouted, kicking Finn into some garbage cans. "Think you're some kind of hero?! Let's show you what happens to brats who are all talk!"

As the two guys ganged up against him. As the larger thug picked Finn up by the throat, Finn turned to see the man he had saved look at him for a minute before running away, leaving young Finn to his fate.

"No…" Finn cried as he was tossed back to the ground and pummeled with kicks. The world around him grew dark, it was like he was being swallowed up by an empty void. And I was going along with him.

"Don't look at me like that…" he screamed. "I'm not a freak… Why can no one else see it? Why am I the only one who can see this world?? Why do they all treat me like some sort of monster?? Why was I born like this?? What am I supposed to do??"

"Do you want the power to live?" a new voice — loud, violent, and terrifying — called out in the darkness. "Do you want the power to make the pain stop? The power to use your gifts? The power to make no one dare to question you again?"

"Who… Who's there?" young Finn called out to the darkness. "…Who are you?"

"Say you want it…" the voice tempted. "Say you'll let me show you. I will give you the power you want so badly. The power others don't want you to have. All you have to do, is ask me for it."

Young Finn's eyes suddenly opened as the world became red with blood. I felt a blast of such hatred and bitterness that my physical body was thrown back several feet, snapping me out of the flashback.

I lay on my side and realized I had just seen something I was never meant to know about.

As I picked myself up again, I felt something stabbing into my heart like a needle. Looking down I was shocked to see what looked like a small twig growing out of my chest.

Panicking I grabbed it and attempted to pull it off, but it only caused me to fall back in agony.

It was as if it had sent roots deep within my heart. One light tug was all it took to feel like my entire heart would be torn to pieces.

What was this? It was clearly a fourth-dimension thing. Was it because I had grabbed Finn's collar? Or was it because I saw all those things without his permission?

I gave a slight cry as I heard Finn groan and wake up.

He took a moment to open his eyes and adapt to the light. He rubbed his head gingerly as if trying to figure out what had happened.

As his memories came back, his eyes opened wide and he shot up straight like a rocket.

"Mei!" he cried out.

Upon seeing me sitting a little way away from him, he scrambled towards me.

"Mei! Are you all right?!" he asked, trying to move his exhausted and battered limbs forward.

"I'M FINE!" I shouted, more panicked than I had intended. He immediately halted in his tracks.

I turned my back to him so that he couldn't see the twig piercing my chest. So he couldn't know what I had done.

"I'm fine," I repeated softer. "So please… just… please look after yourself."

Finn's ears drooped and his tail fell to the ground as he saw the terrified look on my face. The shock only lasted a second though, before it turned to a sad but knowing smile.

"I see." He was trying his best to force his smile to stay. "I'm glad to hear that." Then he said, "I guess there's going to be no covering this one up… We should report this to the police before someone else does…"

Finn picked himself up awkwardly to his feet, and turned his back to me so I could not see his face.

"Hey Mei…"

"Yes?" I asked, trying to hide how broken my heart was feeling.

Finn looked out at the street for a moment before shaking his head.

"No, never mind. Let's go."

CHAPTER NINE

Times Change

The weeks following the incident went by like a blur.

The police came by my house more than once. It seemed like there was no end to all the questions they had for me.

When I thought about it, I was lucky. Finn had come by to distract Matsuda before he had gone too far. But still, I felt defiled in every sense and deeply wounded. Every question the police asked me reopened those wounds.

I didn't want to go back to school while the cuts on my arms and legs were still showing. Thankfully my parents didn't force me. It was close to a holiday anyway.

I didn't want to see anyone, or anyone to see me.

Miyori came to my house every day that we had classes to drop off the notes and homework I missed, but I couldn't bring myself to see her.

Aki stopped by one day while I was out making another statement at the police department. She left before I got back, saying she needed to buy groceries for her family. She had left a homemade cake in usual Aki style.

I hadn't seen or heard from Finn since the incident. Not that I was expecting to. I had no idea what he was up to. Our police interrogations were held at separate times, and I had never exchanged my contact information with him to begin with.

I had my family and a few friends to stop by and check up on me... but he was living all alone. His family and friends were on the other side of the world.

As I thought of that, I felt the twig that pierced my chest digging its roots in deeper. I thought this twig was going to slowly kill me, but I also felt it was the one thing I could never ask Finn for advice about.

It took a week before the police made their final judgment.

They decided that Matsuda had clearly been the offending party, and that Finn's intervention had been an act of reasonable force.

However, that didn't change that Finn had clearly gone too far, even if my safety had been at risk

Save for his arms, a bloody nose, and a few bruises, Matsuda's injuries seemed to be mostly psychological. Since his arrest he had been in hospital, unresponsive to any questions or comments.

I had only seen him once since the incident. My parents were against my going, but when I heard about his condition, I felt like I had to.

It was far worse than I ever could have imagined.

His bodily injuries had mostly healed, but it was obvious he was still suffering from injuries that could not be seen. As nurses worked around him, he didn't look up or move. He simply sat in bed, staring at his sheets. His eyes seemed dead inside.

When I attempted to look at his fourth-dimension form, it was as though nothing was there. As if all that he had been was now turned into a black void of emptiness. As if he no longer knew who he was anymore, nor if he were even alive.

He had used me, hurt me, humiliated me, all to fill his own selfish desires. I didn't like him. I didn't want to forgive him. But this? Looking at how he had ended up gave me no satisfaction or sense of justice. It made me feel like I was no better than he had been.

That blank stare of his haunted me for the rest of the investigation.

But now the investigation was over, and school would be starting again next week. I needed to return to my normal self before then.

And so, I found myself walking down an old dirt road, far outside of town.

So much had happened these past few months. It was strange to think it had not even been a year yet. When I said I wanted adventure in my life, this wasn't what I had in mind.

Still... it wasn't all bad... I thought as I gingerly rubbed the area around the twig.

I didn't regret meeting Finn, or gaining this ability. I didn't regret the things I'd seen or felt. Maybe I could have been happier if I continued living oblivious to everything. If I had just taken each day as it came, without knowing what tomorrow brought with it. But somehow... I didn't want that. I didn't want things to go back to the way they were.

Finn had once told me that he thought the world needed people like us in it, even if we were underappreciated and often overlooked. I was starting to see what he meant, but I still felt like something was missing.

The world needed people like us who could remind them that they were not alone, worthless, or overlooked. But people like us needed something as well. Though what that something could be, was still a mystery to me.

I kicked a stone down the path, frustrated at my own inability to figure this out.

"My, that that twig looks deeply rooted." An elderly voice from behind me said, pulling me from my thoughts. "Isn't it painful when they take root like that?"

I quickly turned to face the voice.

I had been certain that I was walking down an abandoned road in the middle of an open field. This area of town had been deserted long ago, which was why I chose it to be alone with my thoughts. Yet there in front me, sitting on the porch of what appeared to be an old decrepit *dojo*, sat an elderly man with gray hair and a large smile.

He was dressed plainly in worn traditional clothing, and had a long white cane resting on his lap. How I had managed to miss both the man and the large building was beyond me, but my mind had been fairly distracted these days.

"I'm... sorry, sir. I didn't see you there," I said, attempting to regain my composure. "I didn't quite catch what you said. Is there a twig on my shirt?"

"Oh, don't worry. You don't need to hide these things from me." The elderly man laughed with a smile. "I know you can see it too. The little twig that's taken root in your heart. It must have been quite the ordeal you went through for it to have sprouted out like that."

The man pointed straight to the twig sticking out of my chest. There was no doubt as to what he was talking about, and I was too tired to argue anyways. I let out a sigh of defeat.

"So, you can sense the fourth dimension as well?" I asked, rubbing my forehead.

The elderly man cocked his head to one side like a grandfather listening to his grandchild's story.

"Fourth dimension?" he asked. "I do not quite know what that is supposed to be... but if you mean 'do I know about your ears which are attentive, eyes which are observant, and tail which is inquisitive, as well as that twig which has put your heart into such a large amount of pain?' then yes. Yes, I do."

"Ah, yes. That is what I mean." I was trying to remain respectful, though I felt exhausted by trying to track this conversation. "I'm sorry, I've only been able to see these things for a short while, and there's still so much I don't understand. A frien— a classmate tried to explain it all to me, though I'll be honest, most of what he said didn't make much sense."

"Ah, I see," the elderly man mused while twirling the cane in his hands. "And it was from being with this 'classmate' that that seed of regret managed to plant itself so deeply within your heart then?"

I stared at him, a little taken aback. He returned my astonishment with a simple smile, as if he had just commented on my hairstyle, or clothing, or something else as equally obvious.

"My name is Miyaki Mei." I bowed. "May I ask your name as well?"

"It is a pleasure to meet you, Mei." The man inclined his head with a grin. "Please don't let the musings of this blind old man worry you too much. I'm just the sort of fool who can't sit by to see such a beautiful flower fallen to the ground."

He carefully raised himself to his feet and turned back to the front door of his house. As he walked he tapped his cane from side to side in order to find his bearings.

"Wait!" I called out before he could leave. The blind man paused in the doorway, waiting for my question.

"Can I ask you for some advice?"

***

I explained what had happened. About Matsuda. About Finn's attacks. I stayed vague about Finn's past, just explaining that I had seen a lot of scenes I shouldn't have. He didn't press me for any details.

The entire time I spoke the man sat quietly and listened. He seemed concerned by what I went through, but not annoyed by my confiding in him.

"I see." He sighed as I finished my story. "To think that people so young would have to experience so much."

The elderly man gave me a cup of hot tea, then sat down with his own.

For a while we sat there, just sipping tea. Wind chimes sang lazily in the corner as a light breeze blew by. Birds and cicada called out in the distance.

"Um, excuse me?" I started to ask a question, but the blind man simply raised a finger to hush me.

"Breathe." He demonstrated by taking in a deep breath and letting it out slowly. "Take time to think about nothing. Life won't change just by worrying over it… but giving yourself time to rest will give you the energy to face life in a whole new way."

We sat in silence again. It felt awkward to me, but I realized he wasn't about to speak up until I had tried.

I closed my eyes and listened. I heard the gentle breeze, felt the cool air on my face, smelled the fresh air wafting in from the nearby trees.

For the first time in weeks I thought about nothing. For the first time in weeks I became aware of how heavy my heart had felt all this time

I let out a sigh as it felt like my heart was beating again at last. The stabbing pain was still there, but the rest of my body had lost its tension.

"Life will remind you more than enough times how chaotic this world is," the elderly man mused as I opened my eyes again. "Make sure you take the time to remind yourself how peaceful it can be as well."

Letting out a sigh himself, he rested his cup on the weathered end table beside him.

"That twig is a good sign you know."

My eyes turned to him in disbelief. What exactly was good about this painful and embarrassing stick?

"Hah! I wouldn't believe me in your position either." He laughed. "But it's all a matter of perspective."

He pointed to the twig again.

"Seeds like that are only planted when you feel like you've betrayed someone important to you. Normally they remain unseen, planted deeply within your heart. For it to have sprouted like this, the friendship between the two of you must be very strong indeed."

I looked down at the twig which pierced deeply into my chest.

"Will it ever disappear?" I asked.

I was tired of feeling this pain. I felt ashamed to be seen with it in me.

"Well that entirely depends on you," he replied.

"They say that time heals all wounds… but time alone will never be enough. If we merely wait for the pain and hurt to disappear before we move forward, we will find the pain has only grown instead. We will find ourselves drifting further and further away from everything that matters to us."

"What do I do?" I asked, staring into his faded and distant eyes.

The elderly man leaned forward towards me.

He answered, "You must face it! You must face the fear, face the pain, face the sadness. You *must* face it! But you must not let it overwhelm you.

If you run away from life's trials, you will only find more await you when you return. If you obsess over life's pain, that pain will simply consume you.

Only by fighting through the trials and pain, with hopes and desire for a better tomorrow, can you ever expect to see the brighter skies awaiting you on the other side."

The elderly man chuckled a little to himself. "Not that these eyes have ever seen what brighter skies look like in the first place."

We sat and talked for a while longer. Every word he spoke felt cool and refreshing on my bruised and battered heart. I wished I could have stayed there for hours more, but eventually it came time for me to go.

As I walked to the door, he placed a hand on my shoulder.

"Be strong, Miyaki Mei. This world holds many things... If it were up to me, I would wish that no one would ever have to face hardships whatsoever... But at the same time, it is from going through pain that we better learn to sympathize with and help those around us, if we let the experiences shape us in that way.

Find those with the largest hearts in this world, and you will often find they belong to those who have experienced the greatest pains.

So take heart! Your life is not over. No, life does not end that easily! If the incident was the end of anything for you, it would have been the end of the old you. But the old you must sometimes end so the new you can rise up all the stronger."

I bowed to him. "Thank you, *sensei*." Then I gave him a small smile, "I feel a little better after talking with you, so thank you for all you've done."

The elderly man laughed. "Ah! There is no need to be calling an old fool like me a *sensei*." He chortled. "I have done nothing in life to deserve such a title."

His faded eyes looked towards me, as if they wanted to see what they no longer could.

"Minasaki Tatsuya." He added, "That is my name, though I take no offense if you don't remember it."

Minaski Tatsuya took my hand with a slight bow, saying, "I thank you Mei." He smiled at me warmly, "I don't get many visitors this far out. You have given an old man intelligent company for the first time in many years."

CHAPTER TEN
The Dragon and the Phoenix

The weeks had not been kind to Finn. The injuries to his face and limbs, the countless police interrogations, the meetings with the school staff: It was far more attention than he was used to. But at last the day had come when he got the message. He had been deemed innocent.

"Ugh, being a foreigner's rough," Finn groaned, flopping onto his disheveled futon. "But at least it's over now. I can finally relax!"

Finn's rest was disturbed by a loud rumble from his stomach.

"I should... buy some food..." he sighed.

Finn's joints popped and cracked as he painfully picked himself up from the floor.

"Aaa... I'm still so stiff!" he said as he tried to stretch the kinks out.

I guess that's what I get for losing control after all these years...

He found his hand instinctively moving to his neck as the spikes on the collar began to dig further into his flesh.

Was Yamada right? he wondered. *Have I been lowering my guard? Has my getting close to people been putting them more at risk?*

Finn shook his head vigorously.

"No..." he said. *A guy like that would never say anything to help someone else.*

Every word he chooses is carefully selected to manipulate others and further his control. It's people like him who tick me off the most!

Finn grabbed his keys before stopping again.

Still... he thought. *People like him are only effective because there's always some truth to what they say. The question is, which parts were the truth, and which were exaggeration?*

As Finn walked towards the front door he passed a mirror hanging on the wall.

"Hah!" he laughed as he looked at himself. *Like a guy like me could ever be free from his past...*

As he opened the door he let out a sigh.

Just because you can move forward, doesn't mean you can ever escape what you've done...

Finn made his way to the local convenience store to buy a quick meal. He hadn't left the house much since the incident, so his fridge was mostly empty. He was too tired to go buy groceries today, so premade meals would have to do for tonight.

As he entered the convenience store, the magazine rack caught his attention.

"Oh! Is the latest issue of *Jump* out!?" he exclaimed, grabbing the volume off the rack. The store was empty save for a girl who stood looking at the sports magazines next to him.

Finn had just begun flipping through the pages when he noticed just who it was next to him.

The two teens turned to each other in unison as the shock of realization struck them.

"Miyori!?"

"Finn?!"

The two shouted out each other's names so loudly that the shopkeeper looked up from sorting his display case.

"Ah! I'm sorry! I'm sorry! We'll be leaving now!" Miyori apologized while grabbing Finn by the ear.

"Ah! Wait, Miyori!" Finn stuttered as he was dragged forcibly from the store. "My Jump! My Jump!"

Miyori marched on without pausing, hiding the redness in her cheeks.

Once they had reached a hill which led down to the coast, she let go of his ear.

"Ugh. Why did I take you with me..." she muttered, hiding her face in her hands.

"My Jump..." Finn whimpered, looking back in the direction of the shop longingly.

Miyori turned to Finn, "I don't think I'll ever understand you." She let out an exhausted sigh. "And I'll definitely never understand what makes Mei and Yamada so interested in you."

Finn's expression fell at the double hit those two names held for him currently.

"What's with that expression?" Miyori panicked. "I'm sorry! Was getting that *manga* that important for you?? I'm sure it will still be there when you go back!"

Finn shook his head and then took in a deep breath to regain his composure.

For a while the two stood in awkward silence, unsure of what to say, but also not feeling it was a proper time to run away.

"Hey..." Miyori spoke up. "Have you seen her yet?"

Finn didn't respond but averted his eyes.

"What is with you!?" Miyori cried throwing her hands up in frustration. "You're constantly sticking your nose in the business of people you've never met, yet when your friend goes through a major life crisis you abandon her?

What do people mean to you? I can't understand you!" she repeated, looking upset.

Finn continued his silence as he looked down towards the ground.

Miyori grabbed Finn by the shoulder, pulling him so that he was facing her. For the first time that Finn had ever seen, an intensity burned in her like fire.

"Are you seriously telling yourself that you were the one who hurt her, so she's better off without you right now?" she spit out, half in disbelief.

Finn's eyes widened at the surprising accuracy of Miyori's accusation. Miyori simply let out a low, frustrated groan.

"Seriously?" she cried. "What do you think people are? Do you think we're made of tissue paper? Are you so obsessed with trying to remove every inconvenience from people's lives that you'll even remove yourself? Do you really think that's the way you can help people??"

Miyori let go of Finn's shoulders as he continued attempting to avert his eyes from her.

"Sheesh, if we avoided everyone who hurt us, we just wouldn't talk to anyone!" She put a hand on her hip and stared him down.

"If you're going to get hurt either way, it's at least better to get hurt by people who will regret it and try to help you afterwards!"

Finn was quiet for a moment, then he let out a laugh and a smirk.

"What happened to your 'not consoling people so they can learn from their hardships' philosophy?" he chuckled.

"I'm not comforting you." Miyori huffed. "You just really ticked me off so I was venting my frustration at you. If you felt comforted by it then… well… maybe you're more of a masochist than I thought!"

Finn looked out at the sea and smiled.

"Yeah… Maybe I am…" he said under his breath.

For a while, the distant waves were the only sound that could be heard.

"Hey. Have you ever heard the legend of the dragon and the phoenix?" Finn asked, looking to Miyori out of the corner of his eye.

"What sort of chintzy folklore is that?" Miyori asked, giving him a suspicious glance in return.

"Just trust me." Finn smiled while looking back out towards the sea.

"They say the phoenix and the dragon were two incredibly powerful creatures who interacted with humans in their own unique ways. Although the two creatures held similar powers, and both found humans to be precious and fascinating, they fought often and could never see eye to eye due to their differing philosophies in how to use their powers.

The dragon would interact with humans freely. Some he would scare into submission. Some he would aid so they would know they weren't alone. Many believed him to be impulsive, only acting on whims of fancy… but the truth was that he did everything for a reason. Though, he was painting a much larger picture than most people could see.

The phoenix, on the other hand, preferred to watch from a distance. She loved to be with the humans but did not dare to interfere with them. She wanted to see the picture *they* were painting. She did not want to spoil their potential with her own plans and perspective. She also had to be careful, for unlike the dragon, if she fought too hard she would risk burning herself up in the process.

Despite their differences, there was one thing about the phoenix that the dragon envied."

"And what was that?" Miyori asked.

Finn gave a sad smile as he looked at the coast below.

"The dragon's fire only destroyed. It was indiscriminate, uncontrollable, and incinerated everything in its path... But the phoenix' flames were different. Even though they came at the risk of destroying herself, wherever her flames fell, life began to grow again."

The two stood there for a while longer as the waves crashed in the distance.

"You know that was a horrible legend..." Miyori said finally.

"OH HUSH!" Finn retorted. "You try coming up with something better on the fly!"

Miyori let out a hearty laugh as Finn's face turned beet red.

"So, you called something you just made up on the fly a legend?" she teased. "Is that supposed to make me ask less questions and take you more seriously?"

Finn turned away to hide his face as even his ears began turning red. Miyori continued to laugh.

When at last Miyori's laughter died down, her expression became serious as her eyes traveled down to the coast.

"Hey..." she began awkwardly. "Did the student council president say anything weird to you?"

Finn didn't say anything for a while, but also looked down to the coast.

"What's your take on him?" he asked in reply.

Miyori shrugged.

"He's punctual, hardworking, attentive to details, very ambitious..."

Miyori paused, carefully considering her next words.

"But I also feel he's not honest about what he's really thinking. That there is a side to him I haven't seen yet."

Finn nodded.

"He likes to control people..." he replied

"Some have a knack for noticing and understanding how people feel. They instinctively know what makes people tick. Usually this leads to them becoming empathetic, and more driven to help others... but there are also those who realize the control they can have over others and become addicted to it."

Finn sighed as he leaned against the railing.

"For some reason people like that tend to be drawn to me..." he sighed. "I don't know if they take me as a challenge or a threat, but once they meet me they start appearing everywhere I go and won't rest until they believe I'm under their thumb."

"So that wasn't a wasabi eating contest when I saw you run out of the student council room the other day?"

Finn didn't respond but his silence seemed to be answer enough.

"I looked into your file you know," Miyori said suddenly. "I wanted to know why the staff were letting you get away your sloppy dress code."

Finn shifted uncomfortably and his hand began to reach for his throat.

Miyori continued.

"Your application came with a strange request on it. That you should never be forced to have anything touching your throat due to a traumatic experience you'd had as a child."

Miyori leaned forward as Finn attempted to avoid her gaze.

"He threatened you, didn't he?" she questioned.

Finn still couldn't meet her eyes, but nodded slightly.

Miyori pulled away from Finn and let out a deep sigh.

"I wanted to confirm something." Finn sighed too. "I wanted to find out if he was behind Matsuda's transfer."

Miyori's grip on the railing tightened at the mention of Matsuda's name.

"Why would he do that?" Miyori asked. "No matter how obsessed he might be about you, I can't see how he could let a monster like that into the school just to prove a point."

Finn shook his head.

"Pride is the scariest trait humanity can have." He mumbled, "Once a person convinces themselves that they are special… That they're more important than everyone else… That they are smarter, more talented, more enlightened, and that their life and comfort matters more than anyone else's — they become capable of any level of wrong. They blind themselves to the value of others and can only see what they think they themselves deserve."

"You can't just say the guy is evil, can you?" Miyori said sarcastically.

Finn gave a slight smirk.

"You know, I've seen a lot of people do very evil things. But I don't think I've ever met someone who I thought was just an evil person."

Finn turned back to Miyori and smiled.

"We may become blinded by our own decisions, but it's never too late to change. I want to believe that with all my heart."

Miyori looked at Finn for a while as if trying to figure him out.

"Tell me something," she said after a long pause. "Do you really think the phoenix' flames can bring healing and life where they burn?"

Finn looked to Miyori and nodded.

For a while the two said nothing. The wind blew, and people walked past, but the two simply stood staring at one another.

At last, Miyori clapped her hands once and turned back to town. "Then I guess I'd better get started."

Finn started to follow, but Miyori held a finger to his face.

"You stay here for a bit and think about how you plan to deal with Mei," she ordered. "I don't know what happened between you two but I can't stand watching her like this any longer. Make up! Get through to her! Get over yourselves! I'll see what I can do about the student council president..."

Finn watched in surprise as Miyori ran off with a smile on her face. She seemed to glow, as if the passion she had been holding back had finally started to burn within her.

"MIYORI!" Finn called out.

Miyori stopped and turned back to him.

"Don't you dare let the phoenix burn out!"

Miyori shook her head before shouting back advice of her own:

"And stop that dragon from meddling in the affairs of others!" she called out. "He has more than enough to worry about on his own!"

CHAPTER ELEVEN
Reconciliation

After my meeting with the strange old man I started walking home.

The twig which had become deeply rooted within my heart was, as he said, caused from the guilt and frustration I had felt with Finn. Apparently, it had taken root long before, but it was my seeing the flashbacks that had caused it to sprout.

Mr. Minasaki said that the way to get rid of it would be to face the pain instead of running away from it, I thought. But what was that supposed to mean?

What action hurt most to imagine doing? The answer came quickly ...Obviously it was telling Finn what I had done.

I stopped, coming to a standstill in the middle of the path.

No way! No way! No way! I thought, shaking my head.

There was no way I could tell him what I did. I betrayed his trust. I took advantage of him when he was unconscious. I saw a side of him that he wanted no one else to see. How was I supposed to tell him that?

I let out a small cry as I clenched at my heart. Just the thought of doing such a thing caused the roots to dig themselves deeper.

Well... it's not like I can do anything right now anyways...

I didn't know Finn's home address. Nor did I have any way to contact him. There were still three days before school started again. I had time to figure out what I was going to do.

My phone rang, causing me to tense up mid sigh. Calming my nerves again, I took out my phone to see who had contacted me.

"Oh! A text from Miyori!" I felt a glimmer of hope as I looked at the screen.

Miyori had done so much for me these past few weeks, yet my heart had always felt too weighed down to see her. Somehow, after talking to Mr. Minasaki, I was feeling more confident in myself, and I wanted to take the opportunity to apologize somehow.

With a quick breath, I opened the message.

"Mei! I'm sorry to bother you, but I need your help!" the message began. "There's a lot more baggage here than I can deal with by myself. Can you come to this location and deal with it?"

Sure enough, the text message included a map with her current location. She seemed to be near the coast, not far from where I was now.

It was a bit of a vague request... but it would give me a chance to apologize face to face, and thank her for all she had done for me.

I clapped my hands against my face to wake myself up, causing a loud slap to echo throughout the fields.

"Yes!" I cried out to the empty road. "I'm going to do this!"

✳✳✳

"She should be somewhere around here..." I mumbled to myself as I looked around near the path railing.

I scanned the area but I could see neither Miyori, nor any of the bags she needed help to carry. Something like that should have been fairly easy to find.

"Do I have the wrong location?" I asked while looking at my phone.

I was about to give Miyori a call to ask where she was, when I heard a familiar voice from behind me.

"Eh? Mei?!" the voice called out.

I chill went down my spine as I rapidly spun around.

Finn stood before me, ears and tail perked up, eyes wide, a meat bun hanging from his mouth and the latest issue of *Jump* in his hand.

"F-Finn?!" I stammered.

This was not good... I wasn't ready for this yet... I was expecting to have a few more days to think of what to say or how to act around him. This was too fast! I had no time to think! What was I supposed to do? How could my luck have been this bad?!

"Oh... I see..." Finn mused to himself. "So this what Miyori meant by 'stay here for a little bit longer.' I should've guessed she was up to something."

Miyori?! I screamed internally. *Did you honestly betray me like this? Why!? Why would you do this to me?!?*

Finn's ears twitched left and right as he shifted uneasily. He seemed to be uncertain how he should act, and he was having trouble keeping eye contact with me.

I winced as I saw the spikes in his collar drill deeper and deeper into his neck. I had to say something. This was all my fault after all.

If I hadn't been caught off guard by Matsuda. If had been brave enough to turn to others. If I hadn't let curiosity get the better of me. If I had gone after Finn instead of letting him run off on his own again...

I needed to say something. I had to... but the more I thought of it, the deeper the roots dug into my heart.

"I'M SORRY!"

I looked up in surprise to see Finn bent over completely in half. His eyes were shut tight, his ears pulled back. His whole body was shaking. He looked like a puppy being told off.

"I'm sorry you had to see that!" Finn continued shouting. "I'm sorry I lost control... I let my temper get the better of me and let you see a side of me I wanted to keep hidden away!"

What was he saying... Why was he apologizing?

"I can understand that I scared you," he continued, still not looking at me. "In all honesty... being like that scares myself. I... I understand that no one wants to be with a monster like that."

Why was he saying these things? This wasn't how this was supposed to go.

"I... I wanted to give you space." Finn added. "I knew you had a lot to think through after that. I didn't want to remind you of any nightmares. But... at the same time I was worried. I wanted to know you were all right!"

This was wrong... this wasn't what I wanted to hear.

"I am glad to see you seem to be healing." Finn forced a smile. "I... I won't bother you anymore. You can just live your life and pretend I'm not around.

I started to open my mouth to speak, but he cut me off,
"Please! Don't feel like you have to stay. I'll... I'll be fine on my own. I don't want you to keep hur-"

"Idiot."

Finn gasped as my voice cut him off. I wanted to gasp myself as I realized what I had said.

"Idiot! Idiot! Idiot! Idiot! Idiot! IDIOT!"

Was I shouting? Was I crying? I wasn't even certain anymore. My feelings were all balled together and coming out at once. I couldn't stop the flow at this point. What had to be said was going to be said.

"You don't understand anything!" I shouted. "You're sorry? *You're* sorry?!?! Why are *you* apologizing, you idiot! Why are you bowing? Why are you being so considerate?! Don't you realize what I've done? Don't you realize what I saw!?"

The tears in my eyes began to well up as Finn stood watching with his mouth slightly agape. I didn't know what I was saying. I didn't know where I was going with it, but the words just wouldn't stop.

"I was an idiot! I was curious! I was clumsy!" I cried. "I knew there was a dangerous person around. I knew he had been watching me. And still I went off on my own! I thought no one would help me. I threw myself into trouble, and pulled you into memories you should have never had to face again!"

Finn's eyes widened as tears streamed down my face. I guess there was no hiding it now. Not that I had any control over what I was saying at this point.

"And then..." I sobbed, "And then I did something even worse. I took advantage of you while you were unconscious!"

Finn's expression changed as he backed away slightly. My cheeks began to turn red as I realized what I had said.

"NOT LIKE THAT!" I shouted. If only it had been something as straight forward as that.

"I... I grabbed your collar." I confessed. "And when I did, I saw a bunch of scenes."

Finn's legs nearly gave out from under him as he let out another gasp.

"I saw your childhood," I continued. "I saw the people who didn't believe you. I saw the people who turned against you. I saw the people who tried to hurt you. And then I heard…"

I paused for a moment as the malicious voice came back into my head.

"I heard a voice make a deal with you… I don't know what it was… but it felt like death its—"

My speech was cut off as I suddenly felt two arms wrap around me. Finn held onto me tightly, refusing to let go.

"Eh? What?!" I burst out, flustered. "Finn! I don't know what customs you have back where you're from, but in Japan there is a proper order to these things and…"

I felt something wet against my cheek as I realized Finn was crying.

"I'm sorry." He gave a sniff. "I'm sorry. I'm sorry. I'm sorry. I'm sorry. I'm sorry!"

His whole body was pale and cold. His grip was tight, but his whole body was shaking.

He cried, "No one should have to see that. No one should have to know about it."

You can't gain back naivety once you lose it. You can't unsee a horror once you've seen it. I didn't want anyone else to see those things. I didn't want to taint anyone else with the mistakes of my past.

I shouldn't have let you see it. I wouldn't have ever got close to anyone if I knew that they'd find out. It's my burden. No one else should suffer with it as well!"

"SHUT UP!" I yelled, shoving him off me with more force than I intended.

Finn fell to the ground, looking up at me in shock. I dove down, grabbing him by the shirt and looking him straight in the eyes.

"I am tired of hearing you tell me about what pain other people can and cannot handle, and how you can't let anyone else know if you're hurting or not!" I shouted straight into his face.

"I get it! You don't want to hurt others! You don't want to drag others into your own mess! You don't want to be a burden to others! You spent your whole life being called overly sensitive, pessimistic, and that the fact that you couldn't seem to live like others or keep up with them meant you were weak. You had people spend years telling you to just keep your head down and keep moving forward. That doing so was what real men would do. That you weren't supposed to show weakness. That it was shameful to place your troubles upon others."

Still holding onto Finn's shirt, I pulled him closer, my anger close to boiling.

"BUT I DON'T CARE ABOUT THE PAST!" I shouted. "You are not with those people anymore! You are not a kid anymore! I believe you!"

Letting go of Finn's collar, he fell back down to the ground.

"I care about you," I added as tears began to well up in my eyes. "Why can't I get that through to you? I'm your friend! I'm not here for an easy distraction! I'm not here to ignore you and only have you focus on me. I am your friend! A REAL friend!"

Finn's collar began to tremble as tears welled up in his eyes. Slowly the spikes which had almost completely embedded themselves in his neck were beginning to loosen.

"I'm here because I believe in you as a person!" I continued. "Because I want to know you better! Because I want to support you as best I can. But I can't do that if you don't tell me what's wrong. I can't do that if you try to hold onto all the pain yourself. I can't do that if you continue to hide how you really feel around me!"

Looking at the collar on Finn's neck, I frowned.

"And as for your past…" I said, throwing up my arms. "WHO CARES!?"

Finn blinked, taken aback at my words.

"You made mistakes in the past. Who cares?! Is that who you are now??

You have bad memories. Guess what? So do a lot of people! What matters is that you used those memories to make you stronger! You used those memories to make you kinder!

You have carried all those horrors in your heart all this time, and used them to drive you towards a desire to help and protect others!

Do I think you're a monster because of something like that!? Of course not! I think you're an amazing guy!

Knowing about your past didn't ruin my opinion of you. If anything, I think more of you now because I know what you went through! And I know how you pushed through it!"

Finn's guard was lowered, and his mind was a mess, but he still jumped as I grabbed hold of his collar.

"Stop thinking you have to hide who you are!" I pushed away his hand, gripping the collar tighter. "You aren't the guy you were! You don't need to apologize for what you were anymore. I've seen what you are. And what you are is someone I am incredibly proud to call my friend!"

With one fell swoop I ripped the collar off Finn's neck. I was surprised that it came off easily in my grip, and dissolved into thin air as soon as it had left his body.

Finn panicked when he realized what I had done. He clawed at his neck for the collar but it was no longer there.

Much like the last time, the claws on his hands became larger and more menacing, and two dragon-like wings burst out of his back. Unlike the last time however, there was no fire. Most importantly, as I looked into his eyes, I could see it was still him.

Finn cowered and fell back, not knowing if he should cover his face or hands. As he panicked I crouched down beside him and placed my hand on his shoulder.

"You've lived in fear of who you were for so long haven't you?" I consoled.

"You feared the things you could see but no one else could. You feared the strength you had and how much you could hurt others if you weren't careful. You restrained yourself and hid as much as you could to draw the attention away from you.

When you looked in a mirror, all you could see was a monster who would destroy all that got close to him... but looking at you now, that's not what I see."

Finn's panic seemed to settle a little as he looked up at me like a scared child who had found their parent.

"You're not a monster," I repeated. "What I see is a man who endured a lot. Who put others first even when it hurt him. Whose actions were driven by his desire to protect those around him. I see a man who has the insight to find trouble and hurting before anyone else can. And the strength to deal with issues in ways no one else could.

I won't say you've done everything right. What person ever has? But when I look at you can I see a monster? No. All I see is a guy that this world needs very badly... and who has been holding himself back for far too long."

I got to my feet, holding out my hand towards him.

"Come on, Finn." I smiled. "Let's try this again. My name is Miyaki Mei, but just Mei will be fine. Will you be friends with me?"

Finn looked up at my smile, and my outstretched hand, and then broke out sobbing. It was as if the fourteen years of suppressed sensitivity all poured out in that one moment.

For a long time, he stayed there, crying heavier than I had ever seen a person cry before. Finally, he began to regain control of his emotions.

Wiping away the tears from his eyes, he reached out his hand towards mine.

"My name is Finn Coller. Though just Finn will be fine." he smiled. "I can't promise that I won't cause you trouble, and I'm very new to this so I am sure I'll stumble a number of times, but it would be an honor to call myself your friend!"

As we shook hands, I felt a cool relief deep within my chest.

Looking down I watched in amazement as the twig embedded within me began to dissolve to nothingness, leaving my heart feeling lighter than it had in a long time.

The tears slowed eventually until they finally came to a stop. Red eyed and exhausted, we both sat at the top of the hill and watched the waves crash against the shore.

Looking over to Finn, I examined the large wings coming out of his back. It was going to take me a while to get used to this new fourth dimension form… But at the same time, and what felt like for the first time, he was truly relaxed and open around me.

"Hey, Finn," I asked, unsure if I could prod his heart any further.

Finn looked up at me with a look that seemed to say, 'it's okay to ask'.

"What was that voice I heard in your memories?" I asked as delicately as I could manage.

Finn looked back out to sea, as if the weight of a lifetime of bad memories had just come back to him. I was about to retract the question, when he let out a long and heavy sigh.

"Remember when I first explained how our abilities worked? How I counted all the way up to the fourth dimension?"

I nodded, thinking about how long ago it seemed.

"What if there were dimensions beyond the fourth?" Finn asked.

I looked at him, puzzled. I had found his first explanation confusing enough. This was starting to get out of hand.

"It's not as crazy as it sounds." Finn laughed as he saw my overwhelmed expression.

"We know that we are at least bound to the dimension of time, so time has to be greater than the fourth dimension. And then we have morals. Basic concepts all of humanity adheres to even without teaching, even though we can be tempted to or choose not to follow them. So it seems to be something separate from us, yet greater than just ourselves."

"So that voice?" I repeated, before my head went into complete meltdown.

"Each dimension is incapable of fully comprehending the dimensions above it." Finn explained. "It's like trying to explain light to someone who has lived in a sealed off cave all their life. They have nothing to compare it to. But even though a smaller dimension cannot enter a larger one without imploding, and a larger dimension cannot fully enter a smaller one as it is too big… Each dimension is still connected, and influences each other."

Finn let out another sigh.

"That voice was something from a larger dimension than where we live. A greater power than ourselves, you might say. It promised power… and a sense of belonging. And while it delivered that, it came at a price no person should ever pay.

The more I relied on its power, the more I wanted to use it. The more I used it, the more of my humanity I lost. I wasn't even a monster like Tanaka or Matsuda anymore… I had become something far worse."

"So how did you get out?" I asked, confused. "If it had such control over you, how'd you manage to get free?"

"I was given a second chance," he stated. "By something even higher up than it was."

Finn let out a sigh as memories came back to him.

"I'm not sure if you know what it's like to lose everything… To have no future left to you, and then suddenly be given a second chance… but it changes you. It makes you want to live better than you had been. It makes you want to ensure you don't waste your life again."

As I stared, Finn simply shook his head.

"I'm sorry. I don't know how else to explain it. And I don't blame you if you think that I'm crazy. But that is what happened. And I can't change it, even if it could be easier to explain if I did."

I gave a smile as I shook my head in reply.

"It's okay," I answered. "I think at this point I've come to understand that there are many things in this world I still don't understand. And I don't think you made it up… Though you are right that it is a little over my head still."

The two of us talked until the sun set. Before we left, I made sure to exchange contact info with Finn, even though he seemed flustered and reluctant to.

That night I rested easy. A lot had happened that day and I was exhausted. But somehow, at the same time, I felt more at ease than I had in a long time. Now I was looking forward for school to start again.

CHAPTER TWELVE
The Death of a Rabbit

"Hey Finn!" I called out as I saw him walking down the street. School had started yet again, and groups of students were making their way down the sunlit roads.

"Hey, Mei!" Finn replied with a smile. His tail wagged and his ears tilted to one side.

He had seemed so much happier and more at ease since our conversation at the lookout. It was as if he had been hiding in his shadows for most his life, and for the first time realized he could walk out into the light.

The school had done its best to cover up the incident for the sake of all people involved, but it was clear from the awkward glances people gave us on the streets that rumors had been spreading while we were gone.

"We're getting odd looks." I muttered. Finn gave a shrug in reply.

"I'm not exactly used to getting normal looks," he pointed out.

He paused a moment to look at me.

"Is it bothering you?" he asked with concern.

I looked over to some students who were whispering amongst each other while glancing nervously at us. When they realized I was looking back at them, they quickly turned away.

Turning back to Finn I shook my head.

"I won't say it doesn't bother me…" I replied, "but you can't change the past right? You just have to live for the future."

Finn gave a slight smile as we made our way to the school grounds.

As we approached the school gates, a familiar voice called from behind us.

"Well if it isn't the school heroes themselves!" the feminine voice cried out.

We turned around to see a girl with blond hair, blue eyes, and pale skin. Though at one time she had been accompanied by numerous thorny vines she used to grab ahold of every boy she saw, the vines had now been trimmed back, and tiny roses were beginning to bloom around her.

"Tohka?" I exclaimed in surprise.

She seemed to be wearing less makeup and designer clothing than the last time I saw her… yet she seemed stronger and happier as well. She was starting to look like the kind of girl I wouldn't mind becoming friends with and getting to know better.

"What was that about heroes?" Finn asked seeming unsurprised but happy about the change.

Tohka gave a light laugh before skipping over to Finn.

"The whole school is talking about it!" she said, wrapping her arm around Finn to show him her phone.

Nope, I still can't stand her… I decided as I promptly shoved myself between the two.

"Spoil sport." Tohka pouted, but we were too busy looking at her phone to pay attention to her protests.

What Tohka had provided was a collection of social media posts from various students around the school.

They spoke about a girl from Class 1D who caught on to the disturbing intentions of a perverted transfer student. With the help of a foreign exchange student, the two risked their own safety for the sake of the school and brought the transfer student's true nature to light.

"Is this... supposed to be us?" I asked in shock.

"It is not... the reaction I was expecting..." Finn admitted, equally confused.

I had been trying to avoid paying too much attention to the other students, afraid I'd lose my nerve if I did. As I looked around the courtyard, I realized that though students were whispering all around us, they were looking at us with stares of awe and wonder, not suspicion or fear.

"How did this rumor start?" I asked, starting to feel uncomfortable from having so many eyes on me at once.

"Don't you know?" Tohka sounded surprised. "I thought you were friends with her. Our new student council president, Tano Miyori, posted an announcement to all students in order to deal with all the rumors that had formed."

"Miyori..." I marveled. "Wait! Student council president?!"

Tohka laughed as my face went pale. Finn's eyebrow raised only slightly, but his fourth-dimension ears stood straight up, and the fur on his tail was bristled from the shock.

"I suppose you two really are out of the loop." She giggled. "It apparently happened over the break. Yamada Tetsua stepped down from his role as student council president and Tano Miyori was asked to take his place."

"Stepped down..." Finn pondered out loud. "Do you know why?"

Tohka shrugged. It seemed like she was getting bored of the conversation.

"I don't know the details," she said, slinging her bag over her shoulder, "but I'm sure the school has their reasons."

Tohka waved to us as she left. The bell rang soon after and students ran to get inside before they were late for class. I turned to Finn with a smile, as we both followed behind the crowd.

"Things worked out a lot better than I could have hoped." I smiled as I stretched. "I'll have to think of a way to thank Miyori for this. I can't believe she managed to redirect an entire school's worth of rumors!"

Finn gave no reply. He seemed to be deep in thought as he walked up to the front doors.

"Are you okay?" I asked, breaking him out of his trance.

"Ah yes!" he replied awkwardly.

I gave him a doubtful glare, to which he let out a sigh as he paused outside the school doors.

"Something Tohka said bothered me is all. But it's probably nothing. So let's enjoy our first day back, all right?"

"Yes, you should do that." A familiar voice spoke out from the shadows.

All the confidence I had built up was drained in an instant as I watched Yamada Tetsua reveal himself from behind the bushes by the door.

"You should enjoy every moment you can." He smiled, but it was cold and unsettling. "After all you never know when tragedy may strike again."

Finn jumped between Yamada and myself. Small bursts of flames seemed to be starting to ignite on the large dragon wings which had spread out, blocking my view.

"What do you want?" Finn growled. It was hard to tell if he was more furious or scared.

"So, the beast begins to surface again." Yamada laughed. "Careful. You managed to get saved last time, but do you really think anyone will be able to cover up for you if you lose your temper in the front doors of the school?"

Finn relaxed a little as I placed my hand on his shoulder. I was not about to let him stand alone again.

"Aren't you getting tired of us yet?" I asked. "I know I've had my fill of you for a while now."

"Oh! Mean! How mean!" Yamada pouted. "And here I was about to congratulate you two!"

Yamada's false offense made me feel sick. Was this guy's confidence more impenetrable than Matsuda's?

Yamada walked up the stairs to the school entrance where we were standing and leaned against the railing.

"You know, I never expected you to win Tano over to your side." He smiled again. "She can really be scary when she gets serious!

I had never expected that worm Matsuda would last long, but he got you to show your true colours Finn, and that was good enough for me.

Even if he came after me, it would be his word against mine. He was a pervert, you were a monster, Mei was a nobody. I didn't think there was anyone left who could touch me. But oho, that Tano proved me wrong!"

It was hard to tell if Yamada was being spiteful, or if he honestly enjoyed finding a rival worthy of him. His smile never seemed to falter and his feelings were impossible to read.

"How long must she have had to search to find the proof that I had pushed his paperwork through to have him added to Class 1D?" He marveled. "In all honesty I wish I had been aware of her before. She would have been much more fun to play with than you Finn."

"So, you got caught." Finn brushed off Yamada's jabs and turned back towards the door. "I guess they wasted no time kicking your sorry butt out of the school."

"Oh! So mean!" Yamada cried again in his annoying fake outrage. "Why don't you show any mercy, you monster you?"

Finn let out a sigh as Yamada returned to his cheerful pose.

"You're only partially right," he added in a quiet tone. "It seems the higher ups didn't want a scandal like this on their record.

'Negligence in Duties Leading to dismissal' or something equally pompous... That is what the official statement said when they let me go.

I wasn't expelled; however, they did strongly suggest I take a transfer opportunity to another school that had 'suddenly come up'. I only came here to deal with a few last loose ends before saying my goodbyes to this place forever... How sad."

"Ah, so this is your goodbye. Well I can't say I'll miss you much but, good luck and all," Finn said in a monotone voice as he resumed his walk into the school.

"Oh, I am sure you will never forget me." Yamada smirked as he watched Finn slowly walk away. "After all, I left you quite the goodbye present!"

Finn stopped in the doorway. Both he and I felt it... the incredible malice which had begun to rise from Yamada. It was the first emotion I had been able to read from him. This was what he had come back for.

"I was wondering what to get you when I met the most adorable little rabbit in the hallway!" Yamada continued. "Poor little thing though, it seemed like she was all tangled up in a huge mess of wires..."

"Aki!" I cried. Finn turned to look at me, sharing my panic.

"Ah but don't worry about her," Yamada consoled. "See, she was feeling incredibly overwhelmed. She felt like she had to face everything alone. Poor thing, broke her heart even more when I pointed out how deeply her selfishness had been hurting her friends... Well, if that was even what they considered her anymore.

I felt so bad seeing her like that, but I'm a realist you see. I decided to help her understand that life from now on would be just as futile, and that as long as she was alive she would be nothing but a burden on all the people she's let down."

Yamada hit the ground as Finn grabbed him by the shirt collar and tackled him. His ears were pulled back, and the dragon wings on his back were engulfed in flames, but he seemed more desperate than furious.

"WHY ARE YOU DOING THIS!?" Finn shouted. "WHY WOULD YOU GO THIS FAR!? SHE'S A HUMAN BEING JUST LIKE YOU, YOU IDIOT!"

"Human?" Yamada spat. "For all your insight do you still think that we are on the same level as them? The humans of this world are boring! They're idiots! They can't even tell when you're lying to them. What's the point of not taking advantage of that? Doesn't everyone in this world take advantage of power? It's survival of the fittest after all!

If you want to give yourself a handicap and keep pretending you have to look after those mindless slobs, then that's your loss! But don't expect the rest of us to be dragged down with you.

If I was at the same level as them, how would I be able to manipulate them so easily? I can make them give me whatever I want while you can't even get a friend! Take your pathetic life lessons and fortune cookie advice and save it for those insects in there!"

Yamada looked to the roof and smiled.

"You know, if you hurry you may actually manage to get a better seat before the bunny goes *splat*. Last I heard, she had decided to do the noble thing and make it so she could stop being a burden to everyone, permanently."

My eyes widened as I realized what he meant. Without a moment's hesitation I ran into the school and headed straight for the roof.

Finn stayed outside, still pinning Yamada down by the throat.

"Now then monster," Yamada sneered, "what will it be?"

The air around Finn grew thick as his wings began to glow hotter. His eyes burned with the murderous intent he had been restraining.

"Hah! Looks like I win after all." Yamada scoffed. "Go ahead, attack me. I know I deserve it. But the moment you do, everyone will know the secret about what a monster you are, while I'll go out looking like a charismatic, charming example who happened to be an unfortunate victim of *gaijin* cruelty."

Yamada's smile grew as Finn's grip tightened on his shoulders.

"You know how this works," he smirked. "We are only effective as long as people don't realize we are different than them.

If people realize what I can do, they will raise their guard around me, making it that much harder for me to manipulate them. I'll be left alone, considered as untrustworthy scum with no one to play with save for the most desperate of worms.

If people realize what you can do, they'll realize you're a freak and no longer feel comfortable enough to open up to you. You'll be stuck in a living hell where you watch everyone around you suffer, but you'll have no power left to help them!

Your pet has lost her best friend because of you. Her other friend will lose her standing for having stood up for such a monster. You will lose all credibility and be labeled as the freak of nature you've always been.

So come on! Give me your best punch! It doesn't matter. I've already won!"

Yamada stared at Finn with a half-crazed smile, drunk on his own victory. His smile faltered however, as Finn released his hold on him.

"You're right," Finn replied, getting to his feet. "Every fiber of my being wants to punch your smug face in right now. I want to take all of this anger that's built up inside me and pound you until you are unrecognizable. But if I did that, I would be letting you win for the first time in your life."

Yamada glared at Finn, who casually dusted off his uniform.

"What have you ever won by manipulating others?" Finn asked as he looked down at Yamada. "You talk about all the people who would do anything you want them to. You talk about the rank you've achieved. The things you can get away with. But have you ever gained anything of value?"

Yamada began to shift uneasily as Finn stood steadfast.

"Shallow fake friendships, unearned accomplishments, a carefully managed fake image. I can't help but pity you. You've touched the hearts of so many people for better or for worse, but tell me. Have you ever let anyone touch your heart in return?"

Finn's eyes narrowed as he examined Yamada's crumpled form.

"What a lonely, empty existence." He sighed. "You're no mighty emperor. You're simply a sad, lonely little boy, playing with the puppets he has on strings. No matter what you have them say or do though, deep down you know, it's really just your own self-gratification."

"Sh-SHUT UP!" Yamada shouted scrambling to his feet. "What would you know you lone wolf! You monster! You freak of nature!"

Finn gave a gentle smile that made Yamada's anger boil over. He turned his head towards the school with a faraway look in his eyes.

"After a lifetime of reaching out to other people, I finally know what it's like to have people reach back to me. Don't you wish you were that lucky?"

Yamada ground his teeth as he tried to think of a response. Finn simply smirked.

"There was another thing you were wrong about." He turned back towards the side of the school stretching his legs. "Mei hasn't lost her best friend yet. And knowing her, she definitely won't. She's strong. I should know. After all, she's not my pet, she's my friend!"

"Do you really believe that wallflower's strength will be enough to save a girl that far gone?" Yamada mocked. "Do you think anyone can reach her at this point?"

Finn smiled proudly.

"Of course I believe in her!" he replied. "She's my friend! But even if she can't, she won't be facing it alone. Because like I said, I'm her friend too!"

With that, Finn took off running down the side of the school.

Yamada watched until Finn had disappeared around the corner.

"Idiot…" he spat and picked himself off the ground.

CHAPTER THIRTEEN
All Together

My legs were burning as I took the several flights of stairs at a full run. Classes were in session all around me, but I couldn't hear anything over the pounding of my heart.

As I ran, I thought of all the times that I should have spoken to Aki… I knew she was struggling, but I never knew what to say. I was afraid I would make matters worse. But even if I said nothing useful, I should have at least said something!

Aki had always been so cheerful and strong. She was athletic and popular… She even her own personal fan club of boys cheering her on, though she usually denied it. I knew she had been struggling and was refusing any help, but I never thought it would go this far.

I cursed my lack of fitness as my chest began to burn, but there was no time to slow down.

One more flight of stairs, and I burst out the door to the roof.

"AAAAAAKIIIIIII!!!!" I screamed at the top of my lungs.

Near the edge of the roof, lost amidst a mass of wires that tugged on her in every direction, Aki fought to look towards me.

"Mei?" she gasped, her red eyes filled with tears. "Mei, what are you doing here?"

For a moment, a look of relief came over her as she reached out towards me. I took a step towards her, but as soon as I did, the wires pulled her back towards the edge.

"Aki!" I cried out as she staggered to catch her balance.

Aki crouched down and hugged her knees.

"Mei!" she cried. "Mei, I can't do it anymore! I can't be a good girl anymore. I'm not strong enough to. I'm just going to let everyone down!"

"Aki what are you sayi—"

I tried to move closer to her but as I drew near, the wires began to pull her off the edge again.

"Don't come closer!" Aki screamed, hugging her knees tighter. "IF YOU COME CLOSER I'LL JUMP!"

I stopped dead in my tracks. Aki was serious. It wasn't that she wanted to jump. It was that she was being pulled closer to the edge with every step I took.

"It's okay, Aki." I spoke in a low voice. "I'll stay here. Let's just talk."

Aki looked at me through the tears, "Mei! Mei, I betrayed you. You were my friend and I let you down!"

"Aki, what are you talking about?" I asked again. "You haven't betrayed me. I just had some things come up in life. It had nothing to do with you!"

I was trying my hardest to stay calm. I wanted her to see that I was still smiling, but my heart was being torn in two.

This wasn't just a trial my friend was going through, this was an agony which tore into the hearts of everyone around her. But for Aki I would stay strong. I had to!

"I did!" Aki cried. "I betrayed you! I'm your friend and I let you go through all that stuff alone! I didn't even know about it! And when I found out, all I could think of was to bake you a stupid cake. If I had more time… or worked harder, maybe I could have done more!"

Aki hugged her knees so tightly her arms were going white.

"I can't do anything right." She sobbed. "I'm letting my teachers down, I'm letting my parents down, I'm letting the track team down, and now I'm letting my best friends down? I can't keep up with it all… but if I don't then they'll never forgive me!"

"I FORGIVE YOU AKI!"

Aki looked up at me with teary eyes, taken aback by my words.

"I forgive you Aki!" I repeated. I would repeat it as many times as it would take to get through to her.

"I forgive you. But in return, please…"

Tears began to stream down my face as I fell to my knees. I could hold them back no longer.

"Please forgive *me*!"

"Mei…" Aki gasped as she stared at me. She seemed confused and worried by my heartbreak. A few of the wires snapped as she tried to pull towards me.

"Forgive me for not talking to you as much as we used to," I began as the tears continued pouring out.

"Forgive me for getting distracted with my own life problems. Forgive me for not chasing after you when I should have. Forgive me for not thanking you in person for your kindness. Forgive me for keeping quiet when I knew you were hurting. Forgive me for letting my own fears stand in the way of our friendship."

Wiping the tears from my eyes I picked myself back up to my feet.

"More than anything," I stared her straight in the eyes, "forgive me for ever letting you think it was all right to try and carry everything on your own! I don't care if I had to tie you to a chair to make you listen. I should have never let you think that even for a moment!"

Aki looked up at me, her eyes watering. For a brief second, the wires became so slack, they seemed to fall to the ground.

Is this my chance? I wondered as I slowly inched my way towards her.

A swift wind from behind caught me off guard, causing me to fall back to my knees.

The whole world began to move in slow motion as I looked up in horror to see Aki begin to fall over the edge of the roof, knocked off by the wind.

"AKI, NO!" I screamed, and clawed at the ground in a desperate attempt to reach her. But there was no time.

I watched in horror as Aki's eyes pleaded with me to save her. A single tear fell from her eye as she disappeared over the edge.

Crawling on all fours, I forced myself to the edge of the roof. My arms and legs were shaking, and I could barely bring myself to look.

Clenching my eyes tightly, I leaned forward to look over the edge — only to be blown back by what looked like a streak of fire. A sight I had not seen since that day in the alleyway.

I winced at the pain as I skidded several feet across the rooftop. Something had landed on top of me and was weighing heavily against my chest.

Opening one eye I saw Aki's face next to mine. Her eyes were still screwed shut and she was shivering as if she were still waiting to hit the ground.

Upon realizing who it was, I instinctively grasped her tightly in my arms, as if she would be torn away from me if I ever let her go.

There was the sound of heavy footsteps as the door to the rooftop burst open.

"What on earth is going on up here?!" Miyori cried out as she ran out onto the roof.

"Miyori?" I asked. I was confused, still feeling weak from the whole ordeal. "What are you doing here?"

"That's what I should be asking you!" Miyori yelled. "First I saw someone fall past the window, then someone scaling the outside of the building as fast as if they were flying. What on earth has been going on?"

Someone scaled the building? I thought in a haze as I struggled to turn my head.

There, lying face first on the ground and gasping for breath, was Finn. His body lay uncomfortably in a pile and his arms were sprawled out at an unnatural angle, but he was smiling as he saw me.

"You... aren't alone either..." he panted in a strained voice.

"You don't have an ounce of common sense in your brain, do you?" Miyori marveled as she looked down at Finn's crumpled form.

"Heh... Nope!" Finn replied with a half-dazed smile.

Miyori crouched down beside him as she examined the state he was in.

"You also can't move after pushing your body like that, can you?" she asked.

"Heh.... Nope..." Finn repeated, with a little more pain this time.

Aki, having realized her life was out of danger, burst into tears. It was the uncontrollable crying of a child, but I felt no lack of respect for her for finally letting it all out.

Readjusting my grip, I hugged Aki tighter.

"You're never alone Aki," I whispered to her. "Your grades, your track time, your constant smiles... Do you think losing those would be enough to chase us away?

We're friends Aki. Through thick and thin. Friends are great to have during the fun times of life, but it's the tough times when being with friends really matters."

Aki clung tightly to me as she continued to cry. With a stroke of my hand, I began brushing the wires away from her.

"Don't tell yourself you have to be good enough for us." I continued, wondering if I was starting to sound as preachy as Finn. "Don't worry about maintaining the image of an angel. Just be *you*! We've never wanted anything else from you. Just you as you are."

For a while we just stayed there. No more words were needed. Right now, what she needed most was to be held close, and to know how much she meant to us.

And so we stayed until she had finished crying. Until her breathing had returned to normal. Until she herself decided to pick herself up again and move away.

No words were said. No words were needed. But as we smiled to each other I knew at last, she was going to be all right.

***

We went to the nurse's office to have our injuries looked after.

I had some bruising and minor scratches, but it paled in comparison to what I had gone through in the alleyway.

Finn had dislocated both of his arms as well as torn some ligaments. It was going to be a long road to recovery for him.

Aki, like me, only had some scrapes and bruises, but it was decided she would be kept under observation in concern for her mental condition.

Her father was called, and his arrival was awkward to say the least.

Her father was stern and unforthcoming with his feelings. I could easily see how an honest and sensitive girl like Aki could feel pressured by him. Still, even if their chemistry was horrible, I could sense the fear and worry in his voice. There was no question that he did care for her, even if he did not always show it properly.

And so, life continued.

Time by itself may not be enough to heal all wounds, but if the desire to change and move forward is strong enough, time can reveal many wonderful things far beyond your imagination.

Things never went back to the way they were, but that was not necessarily a bad thing. We had changed. But we had changed to become stronger, kinder, wiser, and more forgiving.

I was Miyaki Mei. A student from a small town off the coast of Japan. For the last fifteen years my life had been boring, empty, average. But all that changed when I went to high school.

I may not have experienced a rise in popularity, world saving adventures, club activities, thrilling romances, or anything else I would have read about in my *light novels* and *manga*, but now every day was a new adventure that outshone all my expectations.

To the general onlooker, I may have appeared a mediocre high school girl in a mediocre class leading a mediocre life. But what made these things mediocre was how you choose to look at it.

Every day I was surrounded by numerous people. Each one completely unique. Each one fighting internal battles that usually only they could see. But now I could see them as well.

These may not have been battles you would see on the news, nor were they wars that would appear in any history books. Yet they were a war all the same.

A war you either fought or were destroyed in. A war that each person could relate to. A war that each person went through every day. A war that

no person should ever feel they must face alone.
And I wanted to make sure no one ever would.

Acknowledgements

I would like to thank the Indie Author Community for being such a warm and welcoming place

All who have read this book for being the reason that I write

And for my family for putting up with my creative madness

You Might Also Like

Young Brett Malek had been told that everything in this world had a logical and scientific explanation. How is he to react when he is kidnapped and taken to a country that defies everything he had ever known about the world?

Available for Sale in eBook and Paperback

About the Author

Author, business graduate, voice actor, and all around creative person; Malcolm is a man whose curiosity can never be sated. From childhood, he had a great fascination with storytelling and worldbuilding. Inspired by the world of comics, *manga*, and animation, Malcolm developed a unique and fast paced writing style filled with rich and imaginative imagery. In 2010, Malcolm took the plunge publishing his first novel *Aldenaire* which introduced him to the world of professional writing as well as cemented his love of fantasy world building. Now Malcolm releases *The Wolf of Class 1D*. A very different book for him, but also one of the most personal works he has ever written.

For more info Check out www.malcolmtolman.com

Japanese Words: 日本語の言葉

Anime	アニメ	Japanese Animation
Jump	ジャンプ	Famous Weekly Collection of Manga
Light Novel	ライトノベル	Form of Novel Mixed with Manga Style Illustrations. Often Adapted into Anime
Manga	漫画	Japanese Comics
Gaijin	外人	Foreigner. Sometimes Used in a Derogatory Manner
Kouhai	後輩	"Underclassman" to the Senpai
Senpai	先輩	"Upperclassman" or Mentor
Sensei	先生	Teacher